STAR PEOPLE DON'T ALWAYS KNOW THEMSELVES . . . OR EACH OTHER

★They share a deep sense of loneliness, and are usually surprised and joyful to discover their true identity.

★They are all around us, distinguished by their slightly lower body temperature, unusual blood types, and extra vertebrae.

★You may be one of them. This book will help you find out. In addition to interviews with actual Star People, it includes a complete STARBIRTH PROFILE and QUESTIONNAIRE.

THE STAR PEOPLE

BRAD AND FRANCIE STEIGER

"Imagine the joy of finding out that you are one of . . . us."

THE
STAR
PEOPLE

BRAD & FRANCIE STEIGER

B

BERKLEY BOOKS, NEW YORK

THE STAR PEOPLE

A Berkley Book / published by arrangement with
the author

PRINTING HISTORY
Berkley edition / February 1981

ISBN: 0-425-10603-9

A BERKLEY BOOK ® TM 757,375
Berkley Books are published by The Berkley Publishing Group,
200 Madison Avenue, New York, New York 10016.
The name "BERKLEY" and the "B" logo
are trademarks belonging to Berkley Publishing Corporation.

PRINTED IN THE UNITED STATES OF AMERICA

19   18   17   16   15   14

THE
STAR
PEOPLE

Chapter One: The Star People

For the past quarter of a century, some of our finest scientific minds have made a great effort to discover conclusive evidence of extraterrestrial life. This quest for alien intelligence has fired the imagination of every thinking person on the planet. Thousands of men and women have devoted their lives and their collective energies in an effort to answer that haunting question: "Is humankind alone in the universe?"

We, the authors of this book, have learned that the provocative query has already been answered. We have discovered that alien intelligences do exist, and they are here now, living among us on Earth.

What is more, *you* may be one of them.

Right now, all over the world, certain men and women are responding to some remarkable internal stimulus, as if some incredible time-release capsules are going off inside their hearts, brains, and psyches. They are having peculiar memories surface which remind them that their true ancestral home is a very distant, a very alien, "somewhere else."

These awakening extraterrestrials are remembering

1

that they came to Earth to perform a specific mission. And they are coming awake to the all-consuming conviction that they must do something to help humankind through some very difficult times which lie ahead for all citizens of the planet. They envision that, perhaps within the next twenty years, those who dwell on Earth will have to endure terrible cataclysms, vulcanisms, geological changes, the collapse of social structures, the toppling of political establishments, maybe even the reversal of the planet's electromagnetic field or the shifting of its magnetic poles.

Interestingly, the great majority of the aliens whom we have discovered are professionals who work in the "helping" vocations of our society. They are psychologists, social workers, nurses, medical doctors, chiropractors, school teachers, college professors, journalists, clergymen and clergywomen, police officers, and psychic counselors.

These extraterrestrials have been unknown for years, because they are by no means science-fiction monsters or little green persons. They are normal-appearing men and women within the species *Homo sapiens*. And they seem to have channelled their unique awareness and their special abilities into positive forces for structuring their lives—and the lives of those around them—in exceptionally productive ways.

As some internal triggering mechanism alerts them that it is now time to declare themselves and to prepare the planet for a fast-approaching period of transition and transformation, these men and women are quietly receptive to the knowledge that they have something extra which their Earth cousins appear to lack. The aliens among us know that they have within them the seed left by the extraterrestrials, the "Sons of God," who visited this planet in ancient times.

And they know that they will be among the survivors who will inherit the New Age. They know that they will be among those who rise from the ashes of the Old

World to claim a starseeded heritage, a new renaissance for a reborn species.

About nine years ago, as I, Brad Steiger, was traveling about the country lecturing and gathering research data for my books and articles, I began to make the acquaintance of the Star People.

I remember one particular lecture in a large Midwestern city. I had completed my presentation, including the discussion period, and all but a few earnest men and women with persistent questions had left.

Something caused me to glance over the heads of those still clustered around the edge of the stage and to look up from my kneeling position to scan the emptied auditorium. A woman sat alone in a row of seats in the center section. She seemed to be waiting for something or someone.

Then I noticed a man seated in a row on the right side of the auditorium. He smiled. I nodded in his direction.

The two remained seated until the very last of the enthusiastic interrogators had shaken my hand and said a final farewell. They stood as I gathered my notes from the podium, and while neither seemed particularly aware of the other, they began to move toward me at the same moment.

As they drew nearer and I could more clearly distinguish their features, I perceived a man and a woman of about my age (at that time, mid-thirties), very pleasant in appearance, and somehow transmitting an aura of great friendliness. It seemed as though I recognized them, but my memory could not precisely place their names or what the circumstances of our prior meetings had been. My mental computer quickly ruled out the possibilities that they may have been former students, classmates from my own student days, or home folks from back in Iowa.

Then they stood before me, and I was compelled to stare into their eyes in an almost rude manner. Hers were blue, his were brown, but either pair was as warm and as friendly as the other.

It was not until they both stood directly before me that either one of them really took notice of the other. They turned to look closely at one another, then returned their full attention to me. I think it was at that point that all three of us felt our eyes brim with tears.

"We . . . we are recognizing each other," the woman said softly.

"Something like that seems to be occurring," I admitted.

"It is so beautiful," the man whispered. "So beautiful to come together again."

I had become very cautious over the years about being led into any of the games that people play at psychic and metaphysical gatherings.

It is commonplace for a man or a woman to rush up to a speaker at such conferences and seminars and challenge: "Do you remember me?" Invariably the question has to do with past life recollection and not Miss Murphy's geometry class back in your sophomore year in high school.

When the speaker does not recall a life together in Medieval Italy or Ancient China, the challenger walks smugly away, convinced of his superior powers of recall.

So, generally, when someone confronts me with such queries as, "Don't you remember how we won the Mungo tournament in Atlantis?" I simply shake my head, smile politely, and quietly concede that my memories do not include the triumphs of that glorious day.

But this was different.

I was, somehow, being touched in a very special way. Strange, but profoundly familiar, images were flashing spasmodically from somewhere deep within my mental machinery.

What was happening here?

The man and the woman introduced themselves to me, then to each other. She was a social worker. He was a psychologist. We shook hands, then walked to a near-by coffee shop to have a late evening snack.

We sat in that small, vinyl-covered booth and talked for hours. Words poured unchecked from each of us.

We were delighted, rather than astonished, to discover that, in spite of having been reared in different parts of the country, different ethnic groups, different religions, and so forth, we had somehow managed to have nearly identical childhoods. Certain profound experiences had occurred to us at the same ages, and we found ourselves sharing the full and true nature of those experiences without hesitation. Each of us seemed to know that confidences could be totally shared without fear of censure, mockery, or doubt. We even discovered that we had certain physical anomalies in common, such as an extra vertebra, an unusual blood type, sensitivity to light, unusually keen hearing and smell.

But most important, beyond the extraordinary similarity of attitudes, opinions, and philosophies, was the confession that at a very early age we had each experienced contact with an intelligence outside of ourselves with whom we had maintained a regular or semi-regular communication. And, in addition to that personal guidance, we each had an overwhelming sense of mission set against a timetable that screamed for urgency in its commitment.

When we at last said our farewells, fully confident that we would somehow always be "in touch," I went back to my hotel room knowing that I had a great deal to sort out in my mind. Thoughts and memories were shouting against each other for immediate attention. I knew that I would get little sleep that night. I knew that I was onto something.

Ever since I was a child, I have felt as though I were really a stranger here on Earth. Whenever it was my turn to request a hymn in daily religion class, I always asked for "Heaven Is My Home."

> I'm but a stranger here—Heaven is my home.
> Earth is a desert drear—Heaven is my home.
> Danger and sorrow stand, 'round me on every hand;
> Heaven is my Fatherland, Heaven is my home.

There were other verses, but it was these simple lyrics that carried the greatest impact for me. I felt that I was an observer, rather than a participant, of this alien land in which I found myself. I never really felt estranged from the children around me, but I often experienced the notion that they were like a family of cousins whom I was visiting for a time before I returned home to my more immediate kin. Thank God, I had such warm and loving parents shepherding me in order to make the sojourn bearable.

I suppose that psychiatrists and those who feel that they have some reasonable experience in charting the labyrinths of the human psyche might regard such thoughts as suggestive of one possessed of the creative spirit and its attendant neuroses. But I divulge the above thoughts and those which follow in a desire to share, rather than as a literary stripping of my inner-self for careless examination.

Although I have some rather pronounced memories of a tall man in a dark suit who stood looking down at me in my bed at night, my first fully recalled contact with an extraterrestrial or multidimensional being took place when I was a child of five.

I have related the experience in *Gods of Aquarius* and told in detail how I watched a smallish man with a very large head stand up on his tiptoes to look in the kitchen window at my parents. As I studied him from my bedroom window, he seemed intent upon eavesdropping on their activities.

I shall never forget the anticipatory tickle in the pit of

my stomach as the strange visitor to our Iowa farm turned slowly to look directly at me. I was able to perceive clearly his astonishingly large eyes, slightly slanted in a peculiar way. To my childish assessment, he seemed the very personification of the woodland elf, and he appeared to give me a smile as benevolent as it was puckish. In retrospect, it seemed a conspiratorial smile, as if we were sharing a secret that was profound in its simplicity.

This early otherwordly encounter—together with an out-of-body projection during a pseudo-death experience at age eleven—may have been greatly responsible for setting me steadfastly on my Quest at a very early age.

My choice of a career which would involve a journalistic exploration of the paranormal began in my late teens, and over the past thirty years, I have encountered authentic ghostly manifestations, unmistakable UFO maneuvers, and genuine examples of men and women with abilities deemed "supernatural" by today's scientific paradigm. I have heard ethereal music, disembodied voices, and the sounds of a host of unidentifiable things going bump in the night. I have investigated poltergeistic disturbances, UFO landing sites, eerie haunted houses, and dozens of contemporary seers, psychics, and mystics.

In the late 1960s and early 1970s, I became more and more convinced that these various phenomena, which I was exhaustively and incessantly traveling hither and yon to investigate, were, in reality, manifestations of a single source. In my opinion, the sightings of UFOs, the appearance of elves, angels, and other archetypal images throughout the world signify that we humans are part of a larger community of intelligences, a far more complex hierarchy of powers and principalities, a potentially richer kingdom of interrelated species—both physical and nonphysical—than we may have dreamed of in our philosophies.

Guardian angels, spirit guides, etheric masters—whatever man chooses to call them—all represent the concept of multidimensional beings who materialize to aid man in times of crisis. They may also present themselves to certain individuals in moments of meditation or subjective exploration for the purpose of relaying eternally valid teachings of wisdom and spiritual growth.

In the opinion of the skeptic, or the materialist, the whole matter of otherworldly beings no doubt smacks of fairy tales which encourage dramatized regressive behavior. But those men and women who have come face-to-face with such beings know that these guiding entities are far more firm and purposeful than whimsy or fantasy.

Yet even with this knowledge, as I confessed in an earlier work, the first time that a hooded master appeared before me in solid form, I did not welcome him at all in the humble way that I should have. I tried to hit him in the face.

The materialized entity was so solid in appearance, so unmistakably *there*, that I reacted in a very primitive, atavistic manner. I thought that a prowler was in the house, and I cocked back my fist to give the intruder all that I had.

The blow was never delivered. Every ounce of my strength was instantly drained from me. I crumpled and folded like a toy balloon which has had the air totally released from within its elastic structure.

Then a voice, deep, sepulchral, yet comforting, said: "Don't be afraid. We will not hurt you."

The "we" has always puzzled me, for I perceived only one entity before me.

I know that I received deep and meaningful instruction that night. I know this, even though I have no conscious memory beyond the reassurance that I would not be harmed. One of the most tangible results of that particular visitation is the book, *Revelation: The Divine Fire*.

Divine Fire was an important work in my own spiritual growth, and it has been a book that many men and women have told me was instrumental in altering their lives in a positive way. It is a book that seems to contain an extra charge of spiritual energy that has made connection with many people.

In subsequent encounters with such archetypal forms as the hooded master, I have always been rendered into a state of unconsciousness. It is as though my ceaselessly inquiring writer's brain must be blanked out so that a state of awareness which exists in my Essential Self can be fully primed to take on a full jolt of knowledge from my Master Teacher.

In certain of these visitations, it is as if I am taken to some inbetween universe and am given teachings and instructions. I am ushered into a large hall in what seems to be a marble temple, and there I see numerous other students already at their desks or benches. I can clearly distinguish the faces of certain of my fellow students, but the faces of the principal teachers seem most often to be hidden by cowls.

Certain aspects of the teachings seem always to be obscured. I sometimes recall nothing of the lesson on a conscious level. But I have come to believe that I do remember the essence of the instructions when I sit down at the typewriter.

On other occasions, I vividly recall bits and snatches of the instruction, and I am able to discuss these concepts with those who come to me for awareness sessions.

And it is always exciting when I meet someone on the Earth plane whom I recognize as one of my fellow students in the Golden Temple of Love, Wisdom, and Knowledge. Usually only a few words need be exchanged between us before each recalls fully where we have met and on precisely which previous occasions.

The most dramatic of such meetings occurred to me when I was lecturing at a seminar in Saratoga Springs, New York. I had completed my presentation, and I had chosen to take a seat in the audience so that I might hear a fellow speaker's lecture. Shortly after I had become immersed in my friend's word-pictures, I became dimly aware of a person leaving the row in which I had just sat down.

Within the next few seconds, I found myself abruptly exiting the auditorium, though I consciously wished to hear the remainder of the lecture. For some inexplicable reason, I was mentally being led to the portals of the hall. Once there, I saw a blond-haired woman who was standing with her back to me.

I felt compelled to speak to her, and, awkwardly, I asked her if it were still raining outside—though a glance through the glass door could easily have answered the question.

As she turned to look up at me over her shoulder, a bright white light seemed to flash from some inner source, almost blinding me with its intensity. An instantaneous recognition took place, a feeling of having shared many aeons. And the recognition was combined with an overwhelming sense of a future destiny.

Her name was Francie, and the two of us spent the next several hours discussing all that we had in common.

It came as no surprise to me that Francie could check off every element on the Star People Pattern Profile that I had been accumulating for my work-in-progress, *Gods of Aquarius*. Since the age of five, she had maintained a steady interaction with an intelligence which described itself as angelic, and she urgently believed that "now was the time" to begin a ministry to alert all those who would listen that a New Age was in the process of being born.

The essential pattern profile of the Star People contains the following elements. Few of the seedlings have all of the characteristics listed below, but all of them have a good number of the elements which have been isolated.

Compelling eyes

Personal charisma

Lower than normal body temperature

Unusual blood type—or even a combination of blood types

Transitional vertebrae, extra vertebrae, or fused vertebrae

Extra or "misplaced" ribs

Hypersensitivity to electricity, electromagnetic fields

Lower than normal blood pressure

Chronic sinusitis

Thrive on little sleep and do their best work at night

Was an unexpected child

Although generally expressing love for their parents, feel that their mother and father are not their real parents

Sense that their true ancestors came from another world, another dimension, another level of consciousness, and yearn for their real home "beyond the stars"

Feel a great urgency, a short time to complete important goals, a special mission

Experience a buzzing or a clicking sound or a high-pitched mechanical whine in the ears prior to, or during, some psychic event or warning of danger

Had unseen companions as a child

Had a dramatic experience around the age of five which often took the form of a white light and/or a visitation by human-appearing beings who gave information, guidance, or comfort

Have since maintained a continuing contact with beings which they consider to be angels, masters, elves, spiritual teachers or openly declared UFO intelligences

Had a serious accident, illness, or traumatic experience around the age of eleven or twelve which encouraged them to turn inward

Appear to have unusual abilities which are considered paranormal by their peers and their family

Appear to have unusual abilities in specialized areas,

such as art, music, mathematics, drama, the natural sciences, healing

Often express an alien planetary environment in their artwork, dreams, fantasies

Find that children and animals appear strongly attracted to them

May have "mystic crosses" on their palms

Experience an unusual attraction to natural crystals and certain rocks

Often have "flying dreams" in which they move freely through the air

Have a strong affinity to the eras of ancient Egypt and Israel, when contact with multidimensional beings was conducted on a more open basis by the entities themselves.

In the past, Francie had been asked to lend her unique abilities to many metaphysical movements. She had been invited to attend inner-circle meetings of spiritual groups. She had been asked to travel about the country ministering to gatherings of those who wished to receive instruction in the ways in which she had been taught to contact the guides and teachers.

Knowing that her mission required that she continue a period of isolation in which to receive further instructions in the eternal verities, Francie declined each of many offers which were presented to her, but gave freely of her gifts in individual consultations.

"It was my time in the desert, my time in wilderness" is the way in which Francie today refers to those years of obscurity.

All spiritual teachers must seclude themselves for a time in order to become total receivers. Francie knew that it was not yet time to dispense her channelled teachings.

Shortly after I married this modern-day oracle, I prompted her to write *Reflections From an Angel's Eye*, which contains the many teachings which she had received during that period of solitude and meditation.

Over twenty years of seeking and studying contemporary prophets, seers, and UFO contactees seemed to culminate with my discovery of Francie. Now, at last, I would have at close hand a prophet-teacher whose many encounters with the guides and teachers, and the instruction which they provided, would be able to furnish the fast-surfacing Star People with the guidance which they would need to help bring the New World into reality.

"There exist two helpers of humankind on Earth today," Francie received during one of her channelling sessions. "There are the Starseeds, those Earthlings whose genes carry the inherent characteristics of their extraterrestrial ancestors, together with their human forebears. And there are the Star Helpers, those Earthlings who have inherited the genes of human ancestors who interacted with the extraterrestrials in ancient times or who have evolutionized more quickly than other Earthlings.

"The Star Helpers may not have many of the physical characteristics in the pattern profile, but they are the descendants of those ancient ones who served as disciples of the beings from the stars. They assisted the extraterrestrials so that they might better intervene on behalf of all of humankind. They nurtured the Starseeds produced by the early unions between humankind and the extraterrestrials.

"Later in history, it was the Star Helpers who perfected certain rituals to enable other humans to become initiates of the Sowers from another world. They have steadily developed programs to aid humankind.

"The Star Helpers, then, are highly evolutionized Earthlings, who have accelerated their progression toward the Source and who walk and work hand-in-hand with the Starseeds to assist humankind. From generation to generation, the Star Helpers have always been several steps beyond ordinary, slowly evolving, humans. At this particular time, the Star Helpers have reached an apex before the transition of all of Earth.

"The Star Helpers are what is esoterically referred to as 'Old Souls.' Throughout history they have been dutifully devoted to helping all of life. They very often work through the various humanitarian professions, and they remain attracted to such serving positions today. The Star Helpers are far more sensitive, more psychic, and possess more than the normal electro-magnetic energies found in other Earthlings. They are several steps into the future in representing that stage to which all of humankind aspires.

"At their present stage of development, the Star Helpers can work hand-in-hand with the Starseeds, for they are mentally and spiritually linked with them, thereby functioning on an equal basis with them. The Star Helpers are the teachers among humankind who will aid the Starseeds in heralding the New Age. The Star People are the midwives who will give assistance during the birth throes of the New World and the New Human."

Chapter Two: A Place Like Unto Venus

Research associates of mine, such as John A. Keel, Dr. Berthold Schwarz, Dr. Leo Sprinkle, Jerome Clark, and others, have commented that there appear to be many basic physical similarities which may be found among UFO contactees—in other words, many of the men and women who claim to have had visual, verbal, or telepathic contact with UFO occupants greatly resemble one another. This observation suggests that the UFOnauts are monitoring members of our species who share certain characteristics because they have a keen interest in guiding or in preserving their development. As indicated by the pattern profile we have assembled, the Star People also appear to share certain physical characteristics and anomalies.

It was in my book *Gods of Aquarius* that I first set down a number of these peculiarities.

For example, the eyes of the Star People are of an extremely compelling quality. They are often somewhat heavy-lidded in the manner often referred to as "bedroom eyes" or "sleepy eyes."

The vast majority of the Star People display great

personal magnetism and give evidence of at least above average intelligence. Other people feel good around the Star People and are immediately attracted to them. Within moments after meeting them, strangers begin to pour out their life stories, intimate secrets, and personally vexing problems.

Great numbers of the Star People have Rh-negative blood type or an unusual or rare blood type. The majority of them have extra or transitional vertebrae. Several have extra or misplaced ribs. Many of them have lower-than-normal body temperatures, and lower-than-normal blood pressure.

Although the Star People were born in no exclusive time sequences, we have found that the majority seem to have been "reborn" in clusters of cycles about ten years apart—such as, 1934–1938, 1944–1948, 1954–1958. We have discovered Star People in their eighties as well as Star People in their early teens.

Since earliest childhood, they have had continuing series of episodes with what they believe to be angels, elves, fairies, masters, teachers, or openly declared UFO intelligences. This interaction most often began with an activating incident at about the age of five in which an entity or a brilliant light appeared to them. The Star People have learned to integrate their separate reality with the consensual reality that they share with family, friends, and the rest of the planet so that they may function effectively in the cultures into which they have been placed.

Somehow, the Star People share a feeling, a knowing, an awareness that their ancestors—or, perhaps, their true consciousnesses, their Souls—came from another world, another dimension, another level of intelligence.

Certain of the Star People have memories of a starship that came to this planet thousands of years ago. Those aboard the vehicle came to Earth to observe, to study, to blend with evolving *Homo sapiens*. Their own seed would enrich the developing species and accelerate the time when mankind would begin to reach for the stars—and their cosmic home.

Almost without exception, each of the Star People hear repeated over and over—in their dreams, in their meditations, in their visions, in their Souls—"Now is the time." It is time to remember now; it is time to become activated now; it is time to alert their fellow planetary citizens of the Great Cleansing and the higher state of consciousness which lies in the future.

In the summer of 1978, at the prompting of UFO-logist Hayden C. Hewes, Francie submitted to an encounter with science's most sophisticated new instrument for assessing the truth of anyone's claims—the Psychological Stress Evaluator (PSE). Developed by two colonels in military security, the PSE machine analyzes the subject's voice patterns and indicates certain stress-related tremors which are controlled by involuntary muscles triggered by the unconscious mind. The PSE instrumentation detects, measures, and records in a graphic manner any guilt-revealing variations in the human voice. Its findings are currently being used by insurance investigators, police departments, and both military and civil courts.

Francie told of her initial activating experiences with her angelic guide Kihief, then went on to describe the circumstances under which she was later given teachings which a master relayed to her. She was quizzed rather thoroughly about certain specifics contained within those teachings.

Forrest L. Erickson, the co-developer of the PSE and one of the nation's leading evaluators of its analyses, released his findings that, in every instance tested, Francie was totally innocent of deception.

In a more recent test in April of 1979, Erickson stated that Francie's voice was free of the stress which would indicate untruthfulness. He also stated that her voice was most clear when she was describing the alien intelligences and relating how she is taken to what she is told is "outer space" to be shown living diagrams which serve as teaching mechanisms.

Kihief has told Francie that he is from a place that is "like unto Venus." In my research reports, I have long noted that many UFO contactees have been told that they were really Venusians who had been placed on Earth as babies.

For years I had assumed that such talk of special births were merely ego-stimulating devices, but in discussing the matter with Francie, we have considered that the designation of being "Venusian" may be a method of activating the knowledge slumbering within the contactee's genes, unconscious, or inner-awareness that he is of mixed heritage.

Francie feels that although Kihief may not be from Venus, that particular planet does hold a special importance to Earth, an importance which has something to do with electromagnetic frequencies and balance.

In mythology, of course, Venus is the goddess of love. Perhaps the UFOnauts are symbolically telling the contactees that they come in love or that they appear on this planet with only good or loving intentions.

Venus is also our sister planet, and we might consider for a moment the implications inherent in that term. By saying that they come from a place that is "like unto Venus," the UFO intelligences—or, perhaps, more aptly titled the "multidimensional" intelligences— might be telling us that they come from a place that is similar to Earth, that is parallel to Earth, that is a mirror image of Earth. These beings might be saying that they come from a dimension that is not totally like ours, but, in certain aspects of its materiality, its basic mentality, its essential spirituality, we may well be cosmic cousins.

These beings' penchant for appearing to certain men and women and referring to them as Venusians may, in actuality, be a kind of code, a kind of identifying term that applies to those who walk among us as *bona fide* members of *Homo sapiens sapiens* and, also, as at least representatives of transitional species. It would seem that an ideal program for the mingling of two related species would be to select certain members of the same family and to interact with it for several generations—shepherding, gently prodding, subtly leading individuals whose progenitors had received the genes of a more ethereal species.

Dr. Elsa von Eckartsberg teaches German, comparative literature, and "Psycho-synthesis and Stress-management" at Harvard and the University of Pittsburgh. Dr. von Eckartsberg believes that the Star People do exist, and have been present on Earth since ancient times. She refers to early records in Egypt and Sumeria and by Heraclitus.

"They were always here sporadically, more or less visible and witnessed," she stated. "But now, in this age, they seem, for the first time, to have come together consciously to emerge as a global, spiritual group-force, creating the New Age we all hope for so ardently."

Dr. von Eckartsberg identifies so strongly with the Star People Pattern Profile that she showed us a creative work that she calls her *Venus Notebooks.* "I feel as though I am only an editor of these notes," she informed us. "I think higher intelligences, possibly from more evolved planets or star-systems, can tune in to 'open' humans and use them as receivers and amplifiers of their messages. When this occurs, one can never be the same again. One wishes only to free others on Earth to the same fantastic open horizons and new perspectives."

With Dr. Elsa von Eckartsberg's permission, here are some relevant excerpts from the *Venus Notebooks*:

. . . I try so very hard to be human that at times I forget that I am *not* from this plane of existence called Earth in which I find myself by chance? or fate? or by what other cosmic design I only gradually come to understand?

It is certainly not that I always knew for sure that I am not of this Earth. Gradually, in the course of my life, it dawned upon me that I am too different from others to be explained in Earth-terms. Only gradually—by way of visions, dreams, search in my memory-depths, my primordial desires, my hunger to find a "parallel world," a sphere of different gravity and time and, finally, by hearing a voice from our "sister-planet" in space talk to me most ardently, transmitting a most explosive message —or even mission?—only thus did I awake to the awareness of VENUS in my very bloodstream and mind, calling me back: as a planet I have to regain as a consciousness I have to un-earth, and as a being (a goddess?) I have to embody as long as I have to remain on this Earth . . . living the everyday life people happen to live "down here."

Yes, indeed, how strange this life can be and how easy it is to forget where you *truly* belong, where you *truly* come from, and where you *truly* would want to be—not thrown there by chance but by your deepest desires and choosing . . .

. . . what lightyears of experience-discrepancy compared with the truth of the true Venus-spheres I remember up here in my "crystal-palace" or "castle-in-the-clouds" . . . Why do I suddenly use fairytale-language . . . do fairytales, perhaps, hold much of the truth—Venus-truth—in their humble forms, for centuries upon centuries, without our knowing it? It often brings me to tears to think how many riddles they preserve *as solved*, and how little mankind realizes this. Just think of all the stories about "glass-mountains," "crystal-palaces," "crystal-ships," even Snow White's "glass-coffin" stirs me in all my depths; or think of all the ancient legends, shamanistic in nature, about the "*celestial* origin of rock crystals" and "the highest gods sitting on thrones of transparent crystal equalling solidified lights"—a fantastic accumulation of evidence speaking for the knowledge of Venus-spheres as I remember them . . .

The most ancient Pyramid-texts of Egypt are overflowing with the knowledge or the vision of "crystal-skies" (which the deified deceased pharaoh enters after having climbed to the top of the sacred mountain from which they are most easily reached).

The highest consciousness reached so far on Earth but touches the lowest levels of Venus-consciousness. We are coming closer to connect ourselves—here on Earth—to the cosmic dimensions. Globally, in not too distant a future, we will "quantum-leap" onto the next higher plane of mental development. As from afar, I see the radiant dawn of Venus-consciousness on Earth. It is coming . . . a friend, Ronald studies to become a priest, he is open to all other dimensions of free thought . . . We discussed the book *The Solar System* by Arthur E. Powell, which had struck me by its very outspoken passages on "Lords from Venus" having influenced mankind since time immemorial.

The one passage read: "The intellect of which we are now so proud, is infinitesimal compared with that which the average man will possess at the culmination of the next evolutionary round . . ."

Another: "The Lords of Flame projected sparks of consciousness into mindless men and awakened the intellect within them . . . they acted as a mind of magnetic stimulus . . . they so quickened the germs of mental life that these burst into growth."

An awareness explosion is taking place now throughout the world. People in all professions, in all walks of life, are becoming acutely aware that man is treading very close to a transformative phase, a crisis time in his evolution as a societal being. Some see an Old World dying around them, and they fear that man may be approaching a terminal time as the dominant species on this planet.

All about us at this crucial hour in our history we have thousands of awakening Starseeds, "little Venusians," who have lying within their psyches and within their chromosomal heritage, the knowledge that they nourish a potential far beyond that of the great majority of their Earth cousins. But they also have vibrating within their activated psyches the earnest sense of mission that they must share their special abilities in ways that will assist the weaker, less-attuned, members of the Earth environment to attain a species transition that may be of the physical, molecular structure of the body, as well as of the consciousness.

When one of these higher intelligences approaches one of their carefully shepherded slumberers, the experience itself may serve as an activating mechanism. The very appearance of what would seem to be an angel, an elf, or a master teacher to one of the Star People may trigger a memory, an awareness, a sense of mission that may have been carefully, and literally, bred into the slumberer in a process that may have begun thousands of years ago with an ancestor who was deemed fair by a "son of God."

The seed is germinating *now* within the ranks of *Homo sapiens sapiens*. Whether through the progressive evolution of humankind or through visitation by a more advanced "angelic" species, the world today is uniquely ready to receive the seedlings growing among us. As once Neanderthal man carried in his evolving nature the seedlings of the Cro-Magnon, and as Cro-Magnon man carried seeds of *Homo sapiens sapiens*, so are we now approaching the flowering of a new kind if only we prove receptive.

Contemporary man may be in an unprecedented position of being able to nurse the surfacing imaginal cells for our next evolutionary leap into the future.

Chapter Three: "Now is the Time"

Some time after the publication of *Gods of Aquarius*, we were pleased to learn that James Beal, a former NASA engineer who had participated in the Saturn V and Space Shuttle programs, had become intrigued by the Star People premise and had decided to see if the characteristics of Star People applied to any of the colleagues in his research laboratory. Jim soon found men and women with both the sense of mission and the physical anomalies which I had discussed in my book. He also discovered that the Star People among his colleagues appeared to have been programmed to serve as guides in the transition times which lie ahead.

Jim contacted us and told us that his personal reaction to Star People who were in a high-energy state was a "tremendous feeling of joy, love, yet nonattachment, on all levels." He said that he could not look them in the eye for very long without weeping for joy. There would seem to be an "instant recognition" on both sides.

Jim would find himself hearing, and saying, such statements as, "It's great to see you again" and "I'm so happy we're on Earth together at the same time."

Beal informed us that Dr. Willis Harman had suggested that mankind may be in the middle of a kind of metamorphosis which is similar to the caterpillar-butterfly process. As the caterpillar changes to the butterfly in the chrysalis, certain cells called "imaginal cells" prefigure the future insect and old tissues are recycled into new patterns. It may be suggested that this analogy can be applied to our current chaotic society. The "imaginal cells" are forming and spreading once again.

Dr. Harman foresees a new guiding ethic composed of two complementary principles replacing contemporary society's "fragmented" materialistic ethics: "One is an ecological ethic that fosters a sense of the total community of man and responsibility for the fate of the planet and relates self-interest to the interest of fellow man and future generations. The other is a self-realization ethic which holds that the proper end of all individual experience is the further evolutionary development of the emergent self and of the human species, and that the appropriate function of social institutions is to create environments which will foster that process."

Beal has commented that another way to explain the process of an emergent mental evolution would be the following: "First *need* exists, then comes *thought*, then comes the *pattern* from which action develops. Action builds on action to spread and fulfill the need."

As Beal found more and more Star People who fit the pattern profile, he had to answer the objections of certain of his scientific colleagues who suggested that he was simply investigating people who merely wanted the status of being someone different.

"The people who fit the pattern, in my experience, have very little ego," Jim stated, agreeing with our own assessment. "They have much patience, lots of empathy, are good listeners; and you feel good just being around them."

In an article for *Alternatives Journal,* Beal wrote: "Are these emerging/developing 'Helper' personalities the imaginal cells for our metamorphosis into the future as our needs and thoughts seem to shape/require? We are just beginning to intuit higher patterns of consciousness. Can we not assume higher forms of evolution, i.e., *group thought and need en-forming the solution*?"

Futurologist Barbara Marx Hubbard of Washington, D.C., admitted that she recognized some of the characteristics in the Star People Pattern Profile as being applicable to herself. Somehow, she said, her own experiences had given her "a deep consciousness of having volunteered to come to this planet at this moment of evolutionary transition."

Her autobiography, *The Hunger of Eve*, describes some of these profound personal experiences, but in correspondence to us, Barbara revealed the following:

"I recollect that somehow I chose a specific task which has taken me many years to identify. I have developed an evolutionary perspective based on several deep, expanded reality experiences in which I sense myself to be a witness to cosmic birth. I was both a part of it and witnessing it.

"I saw each of us as cells in a planetary body, struggling to coordinate, reaching out toward universal consciousness and action, increasing in empathy and, finally, linking sufficiently with ourselves so that we would be aware of other consciousnesses in the universe.

"I pre-experienced a 'planetary smile' in which the body of enough people on this planet would be aware of themselves as a part of the whole system born into an infinite universe so that the whole body would sense itself alive. I sense that will be the moment of shared awareness of other consciousness in the universe. What has happened to us as individuals may become shared as we mature."

John W. White, author of such books as *The Highest States of Consciousness* and *Future Science*, responded to our Star People research by agreeing with us that "evolution has not stopped."

White is of the opinion that human nature is changing: "A new race—a higher form of humanity—is now emerging on the planet. My reason, research, and personal experience lead me to this conclusion. And certainly it is not my conclusion alone. Other such as Nietzsche, Bergson, Teilhard de Chardin, Sri Aurobindo, Gopi Krishna, Oliver Reiser, R.M. Bucke, and L.I. Whyte have proposed the same idea before me.

"The grand theme of history is the evolution of consciousness—a story of ever-more complex forms of life coming into physical being in order to express more fully the consciousness behind existence itself. As this applies to the current world scene, I maintain, the many threats to life on this planet created by *Homo sapiens*' intellect-gone-wild have caused such pressure that the life force—the intelligence governing creation—is mobilizing to resist the irrationality of man.

"How will it resist? Simply by bringing a higher form of life onto the planet—a form that will recognize the laws governing nature and live in accordance with them.

"The widespread signs of world unrest and cultural collapse around us indicate that a historical epoch is ending. Simultaneously, a great awakening is going on around the globe. It isn't merely a generation gap or a communications gap, as some media commentators have said. It is a *species* gap. A new species is awakening to its cosmic calling and is asserting—in the face of a threatening dominant species—its right to live. The planetwise uneasiness and social upheaval being seen today is fundamentally an expression of people straddling the old and new worlds as they try to find out what species they belong to!"

Our research received an undeniable impetus when

the *National Enquirer* ran a front-page feature on our work in their May 1, 1979, issue. Although the article was written in a breathless journalistic style which encourages hyperbole and certain flights of fancy, the piece was accurate enough and compelling enough to capture the attention of thousands of readers. The feature began:

"Top American space scientists have made a world-shaking discovery: Aliens from outer space—and their descendants—are already living among us!"

Here, quoting in part, are the elements relevant to our Star People investigation.

. . . Space beings—who have mated with humans—now have descendants called "Star People" who are on a goodwill mission that will usher in a Golden Age for humanity . . .

Detailed study of these space descendants reveal they have unique physical characteristics, say investigators. . . . The *Enquirer* has located an individual who has these characteristics and who admits to being one of the Star People. An astonished medical doctor—who thoroughly examined her—confirmed that she has every trait and distinguishing feature of these amazing beings.

Even more amazing are the pronouncements of scientists who say there are Star People—descendants of space aliens who mated with humans.

According to James Beal . . . the Star People have "uncanny similarities."

"They usually have unusual blood types, lower-than-normal body temperatures, extra vertebrae, extreme sensitivity to electricity or to electromagnetic fields, extra sharp hearing, eyes that are very sensitive to light and an ability to thrive on little sleep."

He added that the aliens also have lower-than-normal blood pressure, chronic sinusitis problems and radiate a strange energy that makes people around them feel good.

He added that the Star People are only slowly coming to realize their true origins.

"The Star People tell of frequently dreaming of a

planet with two or more moons, of feeling that their earth parents are not their real parents and that their ancestors came from another world," revealed Beal— who has met several Star People.

In her mind-boggling disclosure, Francie Steiger . . . admitted to the *Enquirer*:

"I believe I am one of the Star People.

"When I was 4½ years old, two men, one dark-haired and the other blond, came up to me. They were both dressed in off-white robes. These mysterious messengers told me I was here on earth for a special mission that I would come to understand later in life.

"All I know today is that I am to proceed forward with my life and to help people."

. . . A private investigator from Thornton, Colorado, tested Francie Steiger's statement by using the Psychological Stress Evaluator (PSE), a scientific truth-detecting machine.

Forrest Erickson, an experienced PSE examiner, told the *Enquirer*: "She was telling the truth. I found no trace of deception."

But even more amazingly, Francie's own family doctor in Phoenix, Arizona, carefully examined her and concluded: "Mrs. Steiger demonstrates every single characteristic of the Star People.

"Her temperature was several degrees below normal. Her X rays show a transitional vertebra—the beginning of an extra vertebra.

"I used an electronic device to check her sensitivity to electromagnetic radiations," he continued, noting she was 50 percent more sensitive than any ordinary individual.

He added that her hearing and her vision were extra sharp, and her blood pressure was low, and she had chronic sinus problems.

Brad Steiger, Francie's husband—the author of 80 books, including the best-selling *Mysteries of Time and Space*—revealed:

"I have met and interviewed about 60 of the Star People. I found they all had a compulsion to help people.

"Many of the Star People have memories or dreams

of a crash and a great fire, of a period of wandering, bewilderment and disorientation. They dream of fire all around them, of fears of being alone and lost. At every lecture I give across the country one or two of these people come up to me to tell me these same dreams and fears."

Added Beal: "These are people with a strong sense of mission, a sense of purpose. Many Star People experience a visitation from humanoid beings or white lights around the age of five years. The visitation is usually to give information or comfort.

"It could be that there are thousands of them around being born into our species or being activated and remembering their mission."

We did, indeed, learn that there were all kinds of Star People among the readership of the *National Enquirer*. After the article appeared, our telephone began nonstop ringing, and we received nearly a thousand letters testifying to the writers' beliefs that they were Star People.

Some of them claimed to have been activated by the very appearance of Francie's photograph, insisting that her features stirred unusual memories within their psyches.

A June 26, 1979, follow-up story by the *National Enquirer* told of the provocative response to the initial Star People article and quoted a number of individuals who had "openly come forward to admit that they are descendants of space aliens."

Bonnie Davis, a registered nurse and mother of three, said: "My hair stood on end when I read the *Enquirer* story. I have always thought I was alone. I knew right then it was time to come out. The Golden Age is coming. When it arrives, there will be no sickness, poverty or illness. People will live long, happy lives free of trouble and worry."

Joyce Burnett, secretary for a large cash register company, told reporter Dan McDonald: "I have all the characteristics, including the extra vertebrae. I've never felt I belonged in my family and I have strong psychic power. I've known I was different for some time. But it wasn't until I read the *Enquirer* story that all the pieces went together.''

Real estate agent Faye Thomsen was quoted as saying: ''I feel the reason Star People are on Earth is to prepare Earthlings. We are making it easy for you to accept us. The Golden Age will be here before the year 2000.''

McDonald also included this significant information in his article:

> Francie Steiger herself revealed that a mysterious dream convinced her to make her story public. ''Shortly before I decided to let my story be printed in the *Enquirer*, I had an odd dream. In this dream two men told me, 'Now is the time. Now is the time.' ''*
> Most of the other Star People who contacted her ''reported they also had the same dream or a similar one,'' she said. And now she is convinced that it is ''time to start the grass-roots movement for the Golden Age.''

One thing was certain. We had now met and interviewed far more than the sixty Star People which we had reported in the initial *National Enquirer* story. We were receiving dozens of letters each day.

Almost every one of the men and women who identified with the pattern profile told us how happy they were to learn that they were not alone.

Consistently, the great majority of the Star People who were checking in with us were coming from the helping professions—doctors, psychologists, teachers, ministers, nurses.

The very day the May 1, 1979, issue of the *National Enquirer* first hit the newsstands, our telephone had begun to ring.

* Francie's full dream-instruction was, ''Now is the time. Now is the time. You must teach the teachers.''

We had quite frankly dreaded a series of inquiries at all hours of the night from men and women who claimed to be representatives of the governments of Saturn, Atlantis, or Sirius. We also had to consider realistically that a good many people might consider *us* the kooks and dial our number to tell us so.

We were very pleased, therefore, and greatly gratified when almost without exception those initial contacts came from men and women who were in a wide variety of "helping" professions. They had identified with several elements in the pattern profile of the Star People, and they were telephoning to tell us how much they appreciated our courage in bringing such a controversial matter to the attention of a wide segment of the populace.

Then we began to hear a particular testimony that, each time it was repeated, struck a very significant chord within each of us.

It began with the very first call. A psychiatrist in Washington telephoned us to say that two nights before the story appeared in the *Enquirer*, he had had a dream in which two hooded men appeared to him and said, "Now is the time."

An executive with a mental health clinic in San Francisco said that he had experienced a profound vision the night before he saw the story about the Star People. He had seen himself in a UFO, facing occupants that seemed somehow familiar to him. One of the three UFOnauts smiled and said simply: "Now is the time."

A social worker in Oregon told us that she had a dream in which she had been led to a mountain top by two hooded figures. As they stood on a precipice looking out at the valley below them, one of the entities spoke: "Now is the time."

When the mail began to be forwarded from the *Enquirer*, we found the same declaration being repeated over and over again.

C.S., Enumclaw, Washington: "I've always been different, never quite fit in. I have all the symptoms of the Star People that you list in your article.

"Last night I had a dream. It was a very stirring, very emotional dream, quite violent in nature. Then, as if from outside of the dream, there came the command: 'Now is the time.'

"The dream changed at once from one in which I was violently struggling, to one in which I was the leader of a pacifist movement that changed the whole world."

E.M.W., Brown Mills, New Jersey: "Sometime last year, a friend and I were standing outside of my house when we saw a strange light in the sky. After a few minutes, we were sure that it wasn't a plane or a helicopter. The light would come toward us, then move away. It also went from side-to-side and seemed to do figure eights.

"Then I felt myself being lifted into the air. Not my body, but the part of me that some people would call the spirit. I tried to scream, but nothing came out.

"I forget what exactly happened after that, but the one thing that stayed with me was someone putting something straight into my brain instead of speaking. It was that I shouldn't be afraid, that I was one of them. When the time was right, I would be one of the few already here. I was to help with the plan.

"The next thing I knew, I was lying on the ground and the light had vanished. But a few months ago, I heard a voice from nowhere saying, 'Now is the time. The plan will be effective soon.'

"I couldn't really make anything out of this, but now, thanks to your article, everything is falling into place."

M.R.B., Green Valley, Arizona: "Since preschool age, I have thought in terms of Star People and lived always with a deep, inner feeling of loneliness and 'homesickness' which I could never definitely define. As a child I was punished for speaking of things I saw, heard, felt, or knew. I became bewildered and confused that others did not seem to have the awareness that I had.

"I was startled, yet comforted, when I read the list of physical traits found to be common among those who are Star People. These traits are familiar to me, and, in fact, they have often caused some complications in my life. Physicians have often been frankly puzzled as to how to treat my physical needs. Some have been intrigued with the effect that I have on electromagnetic equipment, as well as the effect it has on me.

"The word *now* is impressed over and over again in my mind, and I have strong feelings of great urgency that the time is short. I have experienced dreams lately of very stressful events that loom for Earth people. Over the last few years, it seems that my 'memory' is coming back more and more, and I seem to have a knowing as to my own identity."

During one of Francie's channelling sessions, I asked why the Star People were being activated in such large numbers today. She told me: "The Star People were created to evolve at a more rapid rate than their Earth cousins, thereby, at least indirectly, affecting the vibrations of Earth and all of its life. The Star People were seeded for their particular role long ago.

"Throughout the aeons, the Star Peoples' attitudes, thoughts, creative efforts, contributions to science, and their affinity for all that is pure, wholesome, loving, and natural has affected all that is here on Earth. The vibrations which emanate from the Star People affect all of Earth matter.

"The Star People have always aided all beings in time of peril. They have always caused their Earth cousins to prepare for events which they 'know' will ultimately come to pass. The Star People are receiving precognitive flashes of the cataclysms which lie ahead, and they are gearing up to help the remnant who remain on Earth after the time of Great Cleansing. The Star People will assist the remnant to continue existence on a higher level than they could have achieved alone.

"Although throughout the centuries the Star People have continually affected positively all those in their environment, the activations which you are noticing now are due to an increased awareness that affects those who are in contact with Higher Intelligences before a major catastrophe of Earth-shaking proportions occurs.

"The beings who appear most frequently to the Star People are their extraterrestrial ancestors, who have since been raised in vibration, consciousness, and energy. Some of the 'visions' of these beings have been genetically seeded so that certain environmental vibrations will cause the preprogrammed image to 'go off' with such clarity that it will affect the starseeded viewer from that time forth.

"Other visitations are from Angelic beings, who project images of themselves while lowering their vibrations. These visions cause a positive preparatory effect on those who receive them.

"In both cases, the beings, whether ancestrally from the past or angelically from the present, can only cause a positive effect by their acting indirectly. It is only by guidance and inspiration that they can aid humankind. If these beings materialized in order to affect directly humankind's immediate physical situation of crisis, they would risk entrapping themselves in Earth's vibration."

Chapter Four: The Sons of God and the Daughters of Men: Starseed

This is the way it was revealed to French journalist Claude Vorilhon on October 7, 1975, when he claimed to have an encounter with extraterrestrial beings.

Vorilhon learned that his abductors were the Elohim referred to in the creation story of Genesis, the "gods" who made man in their image. Elohim in Hebrew means "those who came from the sky," Vorilhon explains.

The primitive ancestors of modern man interpreted those strangers from the sky as "gods," because to them anyone arriving from the heavens could only be divine.* It was the Elohim, who, as related in Genesis, created *Homo sapiens* in their image in their laboratories, utilizing deoxyribonucleic acid (DNA), just as our own contemporary Earth scientists are at the point of creating "synthetic" man in the same manner.

In a manner similar to Pygmalion creating a statue so beautiful that he fell in love with it, so did certain of the

* For further works dealing with a physical interaction between "gods from the skies" and Earthlings, along biblical interpretation, see George Hunt Williamson's *Other Tongues, Other Flesh,* and Brinsley Le Poer Trench's *The Sky People.*

Elohim find the results of their laboratory artistry compellingly irresistible:

"And it came to pass, when men began to multiply on the face of the earth, and daughters were born unto them, that . . . when the sons of God came in unto the daughters of men, and they bare children to them, the same became mighty men which were of old, men of renown." (Genesis 6:4)

The extraterrestrials told Vorilhon that the Elohim had sent great prophets, like Moses and Ezekiel, to guide humankind. Jesus, the fruit of a union between the Elohim and Mary, a daughter of man, was given the mission of making the Elohim's messages of guidance known throughout the world in anticipation of the Age of Apocalypse—which in the original Greek meant the "age of revelation," not the "end of the world." It is in this epoch, which we entered in 1945, that humankind will be able to understand scientifically that which the Elohim did aeons ago in the Genesis story.

The space beings explained to Vorilhon that, after the nuclear explosions in 1945, they believed that the Age of Apocalypse had arrived. The Elohim cannot return *en masse*, however, until the inhabitants of Earth display a greater ability to live together in fraternity and love. And they would like to see some evidence that the planet can be governed with intelligence and spirit before they fully reveal themselves to the planet at large.

Vorilhon says that the Elohim renamed him "Raels" which means, "the man who brings light." He has since created the Raelian Movement, which reportedly counts over a thousand members in France. His appearances on radio and television are said to provoke thousands of telephone calls and letters.

Although few claim to have been renamed and fewer still wish to become publicized prophets of new movements, literally thousands of men and women throughout the world have interacted with multidimensional beings who claim to be the Elohim, Space Brothers, Angels, or Light Beings. Whether the year of 1945 did indeed precipitate accelerated cosmic concern with its violent displays of atomic power or whether some as yet unperceived evolutionary mechanism was activated according to a timing device set in man's prehistory, large segments of our species seemed once again to become more receptive to the possibility of otherworldly visitations. And, somehow, the message that certain of their number might be the product of an ancestral blending between Earth Person and Space Person did not seem so preposterous. After all, hadn't so many of them always felt like "strangers in a strange land"?

When we first released information about the star-seeded heritage of the men and women involved in our research, we received some very thoughtful responses.

"I have always 'known' that there were two types of humans," wrote an individual, who claimed over fifty years experience observing every type of species of domestic animal, plus considerable experience with wild animals. "In my very early preteen years I felt that there had, indeed, been a co-mingling of genes, an inter-breeding between inhabitants of this planet and beings from somewhere else. I began reading when I was three or four, and from the beginning I was enthralled by the Roman, Greek, and Scandinavian mythologies. As I began to 'understand' the religious teachings—most of which I early rejected—I decided that the whole concept of the 'sin' of man, which was a 'war' between his 'animal' and 'divine' nature, was partly a result of that hybridization."

C.J.C., from Little Rock, Arkansas, wrote to state that not only did he have the characteristics of the Star People listed in the pattern profile, but that he knew "a little about genetics."

According to this thoughtful Star Person, the characteristics which we had discovered are "non-dominate" traits: "A non-dominate trait is a trait that would not show up in a human being unless, at the moment of fertilization, two of these same traits are mated. If a dominate and non-dominate trait cross, it is always the dominate that is exhibited in the human being. This is why two blue-eyed people always have blue-eyed children, and two brown-eyed people can have blue-eyed children and brown-eyed children.

"Normally—that is the key word here—dominate traits are the traits which benefit the individual in that they help him survive his particular environment. Normally, a person's genetic code is designed by nature to be the best possible combination for insuring that an individual achieves maturity and breeds young.

"The traits of the Star People are all non-dominate traits that are survival traits, and logically, should be genetic norms for the human race. Lower the blood pressure and you lower the incidence of heart attacks and strokes—not to mention migraines and various other disorders of the circulatory system. Lower the body temperature and you have achieved long life and less deterioration of the cells during that longer life.

"Nearly every trait speaks of survival or some other environment when the trait was formed. Do light-sensitive eyes speak of a darker Earth—or some other 'Earth' altogether? Does chronic sinusitis speak for a time when present allergic conditions did not exist—or does it speak for a body designed to cope with other irritations?

"It doesn't take much knowledge of genetics to go on and on about each trait mentioned in the pattern profile. It isn't the individual traits that are unusual, of course. Any normal human being can exhibit these traits. But the *number* of them exhibited in one human being is highly unusual."

Ms. Sadah L. of Sepulveda, California, had more than a casual knowledge of genetics, when, at age forty-nine, she went to college and took a degree in anthropology. Sadah reflected about a very mysterious thing in the history of *Homo sapiens sapiens*:

"The marked shift, usually placed somewhere around 35,000 years ago, from the Neanderthal body structure to Cro-Magnon, the completely modern man with a smaller head, more gracile body, and marked differences in bony structure. There is also the fact that Cro-Magnon very rapidly replaced Neanderthal all over the world."

Sadah admitted that she had a theory as to how this rapid "marked shift" may have been set in motion:

Assume a group of space travelers, who maybe crash-landed on Earth and could never get off, or maybe got isolated here in some other way. Their priorities would be:

1. Self-Preservation;
2. Preservation of the Species;
3. Preservation and protection of their knowledge.

We have archaeological evidence going back two or three million years of a creature evolving on this planet—*Australopithecus*, *Homo erectus*, *Neanderthal*, to sketch the major developments.

Neanderthal was by no means a stupid, shambling creature. There is evidence of some 26,000 years of consistent occupation of certain valleys in middle Europe by Neanderthals—and this during a period of considerable glaciations. There are also evidences of Neanderthal body characteristics to be found in Europe today, particularly among the peasant populations of Eastern Europe.

Even at our present knowledge of cellular manipulation, we are not too far off from the ability to make necessary changes to permit interbreeding of species. So it's not too farfetched to theorize that our castaways might have had that ability.

I won't particularly emphasize the Biblical, "And the sons of God looked upon the daughters of man . . . ," but it is interesting in this context.

That takes care of two of the priorities. The third is a different sort of thing. Their knowledge would have to be preserved in such a way that it would become available only to such individuals and at such times as it would not be likely to be severely abused.

If the "space" characteristics were full dominants, we would very quickly have had the world populated with the space type. On the other hand, if—as I think may very well have been the case—the phenotype (body structure/appearance) was a dominant, this might account for the rapid emergence of Cro-Magnon. However, if other necessary characteristics were recessives or were "linked" in some fashion, it would take much, much longer for them finally to "breed true" in a global population.

At some time it occurred to me that it was quite possible that the "space knowledge" might be keyed to both a greater degree of what we call psychic ability and a greater degree of peacefulness than is general to our species, probably coupled with a fairly high level of technological development. I have observed that a heightening of the intuitive ability is almost always coupled with a diminution of tendencies toward violence and undue aggression. The scientific advances of the past couple of decades are also very significant in this context.

If my thesis has any correctness, a concentration and reappearance of a considerable number of recessive traits in any significant segment of society would be linked to an increasing emergence of the phenotype as well, i.e., extra vertebrae, lower body temperatures, etc.

I have known for more than ten years that there is a very profound change sweeping through the entire population of the world. The best way I can put it is that there is a selection of "increase in the love quotient." At some point, this is going to reach "critical mass" and when that happens, the world is going to be completely changed.

I think even the increasing violence of our times is easily understandable in the light of this theory. If the "love quotient" is increasing rapidly, then it is quite obvious that those whose conditioning has been such that their main "vectors" are negative are going to emphasize what seems natural to them. Yes, violence will increase for a while, but this insanity will only be temporary. A world of love has enormous healing powers!

If I am correct in my speculations and my conclusions, it is about time for the start of the Golden Age. All the "straws in the wind" point to it.

But my considerable experience tells me that things have to get about "X-amount" miserable before people are ready to drop negative patterns and change their ways. I just hope we don't demand that it gets much more miserable before we're ready to accept what's better.

I'm with you. I'm glad someone has opened the door for acceptance of higher dimensions of ourselves and the acceptance of what is bound to come.

One of today's leading, and most respected, science fiction writers wrote to tell us that he was a Star Person and that he first realized it in 1974, when his own "DNA memory packet" began to fire within his psyche.

At that time, he was shown in a vision, "more properly, 'inner hologram,' Brad Steiger's *Revelation: The Divine Fire*" and told that that book would help explain what had occurred to him. He was also instructed to get in touch with Steiger at that time.

Although he did read the book and gain the requisite understanding from it, he was reluctant to contact me until he read of our research with the Star People.

This brilliant author prefers to remain anonymous at the present time, although a current novel will advance certain Star People concepts.

"I wish to hide behind the veil of fiction," he told us. "I can claim that I made the whole thing up. The revelations which I received were so astounding to me that it has taken me five years to arrive at a place where I will even put the concept forth as fiction."

The author was shown a vision of himself in a disabled spacecraft heading toward Earth, a long time ago. He was one of the emigrants of a technologically sophisticated civilization that was undergoing vast convulsions. But the survivors of that civilization feared that, once contact was lost with the home world, they might lose continuity in terms of the handing down of the culture from generation to generation. The solution was "phylogenic memory."

"By 'phylogenic memory,' I mean complex DNA information packets distributed in dormant form," he explained. "These dominant DNA information packets would be disinhibited—induced to fire—in due time, depending either on synchronized inner biological clocks, or on pure chance stimuli. Or a combination of both, ideally. Thus even thousands of years later, the primordial civilization will be 'released' in the minds of the astonished descendants, who suppose themselves autochthones [aboriginal inhabitants] of the planet they now inhabit.

"The DNA packet in a given individual will tell him: 1) Where he is from; 2) What made up that original civilization, *his* civilization; 3) His true nature and faculties; 4) What he must do.

"Ideally, he will act out a series of responses based on the packet, the purpose of which is to recreate on his planet, insofar as it is possible, the civilization which his ancestors maintained.

"I evaluate the current widespread firing of these phylogenic memory packets [in the Star People] as a matter of supreme importance. In February, 1974, my own DNA memory packet was disinhibited, either by an inner biological clock, which synchronized it with disinhibitions in other people, or by accident. It fired for one complete year."

Throughout this book, Francie will be providing channelled information which she has received concerning those who "seeded" the Star People centuries ago. Francie's "DNA packet" fired in her psyche nearly forty years ago. In her case, the teaching visions have come again and again, and her direct contact has remained uninterrupted.

In the interest of a clearer understanding of Francie's channelled materials, I will set forth a brief outline of the cosmology that has been revealed to her and which will be shared with each reader of this book. By so presenting a summary at this point, we will be able to present her channelled information directly to the reader in as pure a form as possible.

The ancestors of the Star People came to this planet over 40,000 years ago. They maintained a physical inter-action with developing humankind until about 4,000 years ago. They came to this planet from a world in another solar system. They were aware that their planet and their solar system was soon to return to energy.

They, themselves, had evolved to become high spiritual beings, whose physical bodies were so raised in vibratory frequency as to become steadily etherealized. They knew that they, too, would soon begin an ascent in frequency toward pure energy as they traveled higher to the Source.

Wishing to perpetuate memories of their world, their thoughts, their science, their spiritual wisdom, they began to scan nearby solar systems for a species similar to their own to serve as their inheritors.

They joyously accepted their elevation from physical dense matter to a finer vibratory frequency.

They happily anticipated their transcendence.

But they desired to bestow the seeds of their transitional knowledge upon others who now were as they had been, and, thereby, aid those others to develop spiritually. It had taken their species many thousands of years to evolve toward this high spiritual state. Although humankind would eventually reach transcendence—the natural and eventual goal of all creation—their starseed would accelerate the process for the dwellers of Earth.

Although the Sowers were still in the physical form when their Starships arrived on Earth, they were rapidly rising in vibration. They were immediately considered as gods by primitive humankind, and the ability of certain of the more finely etherealized Sowers to disregard the physical limitations of time and space and matter left no questions as to their divine nature.

So it was that the "sons and daughters of God" physically interacted with the strongest and the most attractive of the sons and daughters of man.

The DNA memory packet, with its longings for the true home in the stars, its knowledge of how to fashion a progressive civilization, its awareness that man may one day transcend the physical, its sense of mission as to what must be done to accelerate evolution toward the Source, was seeded within the progeny which were derived from those early unions. Whether this was accomplished by actual sexual intercourse or the enrichment of *Homo sapiens* sperm and egg by technological expertise—or a combination of the two—is unimportant. The first "giants" in the Earth were born.

By about 2000 B. C. all but a very few of the Sowers had transcended to a higher dimension of reality, progressing ever upward in vibration toward the Source.

The Sowers may still lower their frequency if they choose and enter again the three-dimensional reality of Earth. They may appear to their Starseeded descendants in order to relay teachings or to provide guidance; but they cannot remain physical for very long, or they may again find themselves trapped in the lower vibration.

Because of their apparent ability to come and go in the twinkling of an eye without regard for ceilings or walls, they are often thought to be angels. Although the Sowers may serve in that traditional capacity, the true angels are in a dimension of even higher vibration. The Sowers are better referred to as Light Beings.

The Higher Angelic Realm contains spiritual entities who have never known a physical existence on any three-dimensional world. The true "messengers of God" who serve as guides to Earthlings and to extraterrestrials alike come from the Lower Angelic Realm.

Francie's visions and channelled teachings have convinced her that, just as the Bible states, there truly are powers and principalities which exist in other dimensions all around us. Her glimpses of the in-between universes have also made her very much aware that we are all multidimensional beings. Each of us has an aspect of himself or herself that exists on other levels of the Greater Reality.

The difference between those who bear the starseed and those who do not is that the Star People are aware that they are citizens of more than one universe, more than one level of being, more than one dimensional essence.

Chapter Five: The Starbirth Questionnaire

To facilitate our research, we developed the following questionnaire. The reader may be interested in responding to the various items and in analyzing his or her own Star Person potential.

The pattern profile of the Star People contains the following elements. Check those to which you relate:

1. Unusual blood type____.
2. Lower body temperature____.
3. Low blood pressure____.
4. Extra or transitional vertebrae____.
5. Check in which areas you are hypersensitive: pain____, light____, touch____, smell____, hearing____, taste____, emotion____.
6. Do you require much sleep____ or little sleep____?
7. Were you a favorite child____, unliked child____, unwanted child____?
8. Did you suffer from chronic sinusitis? Yes____, no____.
9. Do you suffer from swollen and painful joints____, headaches seemingly brought on by humidity____, a

severe pain in the back of your neck____?

10. Did you feel your father and mother were not your true parents?____ Have you often felt that your true ancestors came from another world?____ Have you often yearned for a place you consider to be your true home?____

11. Do you experience a feeling of great urgency in which you feel you have only a short time to complete important, though often not clearly realized goals?____

12. Did you have unseen friends as a child?____

13. Do you often hear a whine, a click, a buzzing sound preceding or during psychic events?____

14. Check which applies to you: I do my best physical labor in the day and my best mental labor at night____. I do my best physical labor at night and my best mental labor in the day____.

15. Did it seem as though you had unusual natural ability for any of the following:
art____, music____, mathematics____, healing____, acting____, inventions____?

16. Have you ever been told that you have unusual or compelling eyes?____

17. Check those items to which you seem to have a more than normal attraction:
willow trees____, hummingbirds____, eagles____, rocks____, stars____, lilacs____, natural crystals____, mushrooms____, darkness____, electrical storms____, nature____, the name Leah or Lia (Lee-ah)____.

18. Do you feel any sort of attachment to the planet Venus?____

19. Is it true or not that you seem to be an "empath," taking on the problems, feelings, pains of those around you?____

20. Do you often see a bright light even when your eyes are closed?____

21. Have you received the message from your guidance, "Now is the Time"?____

22. Are you attracted to the constellation Sirius____, Drago____, other (please indicate which)

_____.

23. Do you believe in reincarnation?____

If you feel that you remember one or more past lives,

indicate which countries they were in and in which time period they transpired:_____.

24. If you have a pet, please indicate the type and its breed: _____.

25. State your preference for your favorite type of music_____, books_____, movies_____, humor_____, television viewing_____.

26. State your attitude toward death: _____
_____

27. Have you ever taken hallucinogenic or psychotropic drugs?_____

28. Please state in brief the event that occurred to you around the age of five. Tell who or what you saw. Please share what message, if any, was given: _____.

29. Please state in brief the event that occurred to you around the age of eleven that altered your lifestyle or your attitudes:_____
_____.

30. If you have maintained contact with an entity or entities, how is that contact made? _____

31. What do your entities look like?_____

32. What types of messages do you receive?
_____

33. When do you feel the following events will take place? Pole shift_____, global famine_____, WW III_____, "Armageddon"_____, worldwide UFO contact_____, The New Age_____, the first of the dramatic Earth Changes_____.

If you mentally answered the above questions or if you took the trouble to write down your answers on a separate sheet of paper, you might enjoy comparing your responses with the analysis of the questionnaires which we have received from the Star People around the world. Please understand that this aspect of our work is definitely "in-progress" since we are steadily being contacted by those men and women who feel that they fit the pattern profile and who wish to assist us in our work by completing a questionnaire. Percentages given, therefore, are based on respondents as of January 1980, and it is difficult to predict whether subsequent input will alter the present standings.

From the initial flood of letters sent to us by those people who responded with interest or identification with our research, we selected several hundred men and women to whom we decided to send the above questionnaire. Our criteria focused on what we could judge from the person's query as to his or her potential as a Star Person and his or her sincerity.

As we stand now with the continuing inflow of questionnaires, we consider 36 % of our respondents to be Starseed; 47% to be Star Helpers; and 17% to be men and women obviously fascinated by our work and, quite probably, evolving toward increased awareness.

According to the questionnaires, 10.5% of the respondents have extra or transitional vertebrae; 15% have an unusual blood type; 10.5% have both an extra vertebra and an unusual blood type.

The following percentages are based solely on the Starseeds' responses:

Slightly more than 92% have a lower-than-normal body temperature.

Low blood pressure is a trait of 73%.

The Starseed are most sensitive to . . . light, 84%; touch, 77%; and emotion, 84%.

At this point in our research, the initial claims of the Starseeds' ability to function on little sleep does not appear to be shared by all of them. We find the percentages almost equally divided among the Starseed who require much sleep and those who thrive on little sleep.

Interestingly, while 43% of the Starseed believed that they were favorite children in their respective families, an astonishing 92% felt that their father and mother were not their true parents.

Although chronic sinusitis at first appeared to be almost a requirement to be among the Starseed, larger numbers of questionnaires indicate that about 65% of the extraterrestrial progeny are troubled by chronic sinusitis.

At the same time, 46% suffer from swollen and painful joints; 69% must endure pain in the back of the neck; and 60% are adversely affected by high humidity.

Alien ancestors have always been suspected by 81% of the Starseed, and they emphasize that they had these suspicions long before they read of our research.

A startling 96% of the Starseed insist that they have always yearned for a place that they consider their "true home," somewhere not on Earth.

About 89% of the Starseed experience an inner feeling of great urgency, and 80% of them envision themselves as working against some cosmic timetable in order to complete important goals. Some of the Starseed express additional tension when they admit that they have not yet received a clear image of precisely what their goal is to be.

In addition to the activating visitation of angel, elf, or Light Being at around age of five, 80% of the Starseed admit to having had other unseen friends as children.

We were really quite amazed when we tabulated that slightly more than 77% of the Starseed heard a whine, a clicking, or a buzzing sound preceding or during psychic events.

The Starseed are overwhelmingly "night people," with 84% indicating that they prefer doing their important mental work after sundown.

Our questionnaire permitted each respondent to check more than one "unusual natural ability." The Starseed testified to their pronounced abilities in the following percentages: art, 53%; music, 65%; mathematics, 26%; healing, 65%; acting, 42%; inventions, 53%.

Of the Starseed we have tabulated thus far, 84% have unusual or compelling eyes, and 88% consider themselves to be natural "empaths," who take on the problems, feelings, and pains of those around them.

The preferences for the items of "more than normal attraction and affinity" were quite scattered, as might be expected. We included the various subjects on the list because so many of our early letters from alleged Star People mentioned certain topics over and over, in a kind of repetitiousness that we felt had to be more than coincidence.

We are certain that each of the items is in some way symbolical. The affinity for willow trees may indicate a desire to be pliant and flexible in relationships with other people. The eagle may represent a wish to soar high toward the heavens and toward the true home. The Starseed appear so fond of natural crystals that we feel all kinds of memory links must be activated by the crystal necklaces, pendants, and pins which they wear.

At this time, among the more frequently selected items, 61% of the Starseed are drawn to willow trees; 69% to eagles; 69% to rocks; 92% to stars; 71% to lilacs; 88% to natural crystals; 76% to electrical storms; 96% to nature. As the percentages indicate, most of the respondents check several subjects.

A special note about the name Leah or Lia: We found that this name surfaced again and again in our personal consultations with the Starseed, so we included it on the questionnaire to see how many might respond to it. Thus far, the name has meaning to 53% of the Starseed.

We are not at all certain what it means, but 92% of the Starseed often see a bright light when their eyes are closed.

Not all of the Starseed have been alerted that "Now is the Time," but 73% of them have, and they are eager to begin completing their missions.

At this time, the greatest number of respondents are attracted to the constellation Sirius.

Not all of the Starseed claim to remember past lives, but 100% of them believe in reincarnation.

Those who listed countries in which they felt they

might have had previous life experiences have named Egypt the most often. Numerous other countries were mentioned in lesser percentages, i.e., ancient England, revolutionary France, ancient Israel.

Nearly all of the Starseed enjoy pets, and we find them about equally divided between cat lovers and dog lovers. Some supplement their households with birds; a few appreciate reptilian pets.

Classical music is the favorite of 58% of the Starseed.

It did not surprise us that 58% of them preferred metaphysical books to read. We were also prepared for the fact that science fiction reading is their second choice.

Science fiction is number one at the movies for the Starseed. Comedy is second.

Their sense of humor tends to be satirical in nature, according to the largest number of designations on the questionnaire.

Television viewing is composed most often of talk shows, documentaries, and science fiction.

Death does not disturb very many of the Starseed, for 88% regard it as merely a transition or a graduation process.

An overwhelming number of the Starseed have resisted the highly popularized allure of hallucinogenic drugs. According to the responses on the questionnaire, 90% state that they have never tried any of the offerings of the drug scene.

The Starseed have all had the activating vision at about the age of five, and most have endured a traumatic event around the age of eleven. The great majority of them have maintained at least a sporadic contact with a guiding entity and have continued to receive messages and visions at various times in their lives.

Not all of the Starseed feel endowed with the gift of prophecy, and we were aware of that fact before we asked the question about their "feelings" regarding the dates for the various earthshaking events. Herewith is a consensus of those Starseed who responded to our request:

A pole shift may begin from 1982–1984.

A worldwide famine has already begun and will worsen in 1982.

World War III may break out in the period of 1982 to 1985.

Armageddon, the last great battle between Good and Evil, will begin in 1989 or 1990.

Worldwide UFO contact is quietly beginning now and will continue toward its apex in 1986.

The New Age has already begun and will have its "ups" and "downs" until the year 2000.

The Earth Changes have begun, but will sporadically shudder the planet in earnest from 1984 until the end of the century.

If any reader should wish to participate in this continuing research or wish to determine if he or she might be Starseed or Star Helper, information and questionnaires may be obtained by writing to Francie and Brad Steiger, P.O. Box 22006, Phoenix, AZ 85028.

Chapter Six: The Activating Experience

As Francie told the story in *Reflections from an Angel's Eye*, Kihief, her angelic guide, first appeared to her when she was about five years old. Although her father was also present in the room, occupied with hanging a picture, and her mother was working in a nearby room, Francie alone heard the message and received the activating vision of the angel.

To quote briefly from Francie's experience, she states that the entity appeared coming slowly down into the bedroom, directly through the ceiling:

"He alighted so gently . . . I wasn't certain that he ever touched the floor. His white robe was draped over one shoulder, and the wind [from an open window] made it flow in and out around his body. His hair was straw-colored and straight, and was styled in a pageboy cut, coming down to the base of his neck. His eyes were light, wide-set; he had a large, full jaw and fair skin. There appeared to be no beard-growth area . . .

"He began to speak, rising and falling in tone, as one would sing and talk at the same time in a falsetto voice."

54

Francie pleaded for her father to take notice of the angel, but it was as if he were frozen in suspended animation.

Now, in addition to the blond-haired male angel in the center of the room, each of the four corners were now filled with the face of an angelic being. In direct contrast to the Nordic-type angel, the four newcomers appeared to be female, much darker in complexion, with smaller features, dark eyes, and long, very dark, wavy hair. They made no sound, but looked on with smiling faces.

The angel told Francie that she must listen to his every utterance. When she nervously disobeyed and continued to attempt to gain her parents' attention, the angel's gentle, high-pitched singing voice was suddenly replaced by a low, harsh monotone that seemed almost mechanical. "Do not tell your parents!" the angel scolded her.

The blond entity continued to sing-talk to Francie until he and the four dark-complexioned female angels slowly faded away.

One of the phrases which Kihief repeated, and one that particularly puzzled the unchurched five-year-old girl, was, "Like unto another Christ child you will be."

"First of all, Kihief did not say that I *was* the Christ child or even *another* Christ child," Francie has emphasized. "He said that I was 'like unto' another Christ child. This may mean that I will function on a similar spiritual vibration to elevate the awareness of others. It may also mean that I will have certain tasks to perform in this 'Christ' vibration.

"All sincere spiritual workers and seekers may attune themselves to the Christ vibration," she added. "And I know that there exist others on Earth now with a mission similar to mine."

[Included in Forrest Erickson's Psychological Stress Evaluator analysis of Francie's interview are the following assessments:

Francie: "The angel was coming down through the ceiling."
Evaluation: True.
Francie: "The angel told me, 'Like unto another Christ child you will be.' "
Evaluation: True. This is very true.]

Francie remembered consciously a great deal of what Kihief told her at that time. Interestingly, other bits of the revelation are only now beginning to surface.

Although her parents have both come to accept the validity of Francie's experiences, at the time, the five-year-old's testimony did not receive a particularly warm reception.

"My mother had been troubled since my infancy with my differences, my various visions, my 'thousand-year-old eyes,' my dreams, and my predictions," Francie recalled.

"Mother's response was typical of an attitude that prevailed in those days—and, regretfully, still survives today—that such gifts, abilities, and visions belong not to God. I can remember her taking me to a large neighborhood Methodist church and having the reverend and his wife put their hands on me and kneel down, praying for my soul."

Francie has since been told in meditation that the reason that she had the vision of Kihief was to activate her to the mission that she is to help bring as many souls as possible to a higher state of awareness. Throughout her life, therefore, she has endeavored to give the energy of unconditional love and to counsel only of spiritual matters to those men and women who have come to her for help.

From the moment of that first activating visionary experience, Francie has maintained a continual interaction with Kihief.

I have witnessed Kihief providing her with profound spiritual truths and with such practical information as specific names of men and women with whom we needed to come into contact. In strange cities, he has given us correct street addresses and guided us through busy and crowded traffic lanes to the home or business place which we have been seeking.

Francie's great teaching visions come from another entity, however. She has never learned his name, but he is dark-complexioned, berobed, and stern in demeanor. This Master Teacher takes her out-of-the-body and leaves her suspended somewhere in "outer space." It is in this "inbetween universe" that Francie is presented with living diagrams, which she must interpret both literally and symbolically when she returns to the three-dimensional Earth plane of existence.

[From the PSE evaluation:

Francie: "I have felt continual interaction with these (angelic) beings."

Evaluation: True.

Francie: "I am taken out of the body and shown visions."

Evaluation: That appears true.

Francie: "I am taken to outer space and presented with teachings."

Evaluation: This is some of the least stress we have seen during the entire test.

Francie's description of the angelic entities as being larger than humankind, very muscular, and exceedingly attractive was evaluated in this way: Some doubt expressed that they were taller. It is true that they were muscular in appearance and not thin at all. *Essentially, all her statements appear true.*]

As we examine more and more of the questionnaires submitted by the Star People, we learn that the great majority of them had an activating experience with an entity of some kind at about the age of five. In many cases, an intimate and continuing interaction was established at the very moment of this initial contact.

Sometimes, regrettably, the valued guidance has been lost. But in the lives of a sizeable percentage of the Star People, a steady, reliable communication remains a comforting reality in their lives.

Dr. G.H., clinical and child psychologist, Texas: "I saw my first angel at about age six. I saw my deceased sister the night of her death and talked with her. I have since spoken with many so-called deceased. I had one experience with a blinding white light, many clairvoyant and precognitive events. I have seen many entities of many different types."

C.L., special education teacher, doctoral candidate, Arizona: "When I was about the age of five, an entity came out of the sunset in so brilliant a light that I remember putting up my hand to shade my eyes. He definitely appeared to be an American Indian, and he said, 'Go toward the sunset.' I seemed to know my destiny lay there. For that reason, I am in Arizona today. That blanket-robed individual has followed me around. He has been with me all the time."

Barbara May, professional astrologer, Arizona: "At the age of five, I was sitting alone in a field of flowers in California, when the entire field became a brilliant light. I was looking at my hands, and a feeling of not belonging came over me. I was frightened, and I thought to myself, 'What am I doing here?'

"After attending a Dick and Trenna Sutphen seminar in July of 1976, I learned, through hypnosis, the names of those [entities] who were there in the field that day. Contact is now made through the use of the trigger question or self-induced hypnosis. I channel an entity named Thaleda (the one who seems there most of the time), another named Ninian, who is aware of his multidimensional personality, and, on rare occasions, Omnia, who, I think, is the master soul. I see Thaleda as a deep purple light—though when channelling I've been told I change physically and 'she' has long, blond hair and a face similar, yet different from, mine. Ninian is a youth with reddish skin. Omnia is a rainbow of flashing and moving lights.''

J.H., artist, Colorado: "At age five or six, I saw an angelic bearded figure in my front yard. He told me I would be a leader in later life. The figure was enveloped by bright light. I began to sing.

"At age fourteen, I was visiting relatives in Missouri. The entity appeared and told me that I could play the guitar. And I could!

"At age fifteen, I came home from church to find my father dead in the bedroom. I did not cry, for I knew then that we must accept death as a transcendence to spiritual life. At sixteen, I had a premonition that my sister would die in an automobile accident. I was prepared for her death because of my established faith.

"I have had many dreams and visions since that time (I am now twenty-eight). My latest dreams have been of the being I saw at the age of five, telling me 'not to worry, to be patient.' My time will come."

S.S., psychotherapist, New York: "At age five, an ethereal female figure appeared at the foot of my bed. This entity frightened me into leaving the room. There were gunshots outside of the house which ricocheted into my bed. Had I remained there, I would have been killed.

"Since the age of fourteen, I have identified this ethereal female figure as a 'Mother Goddess' I recognize as Bast. Contact is made through meditation now, but she has also appeared spontaneously. I *hear* her. She guides me, scolds me, corrects. Recently, I have felt her massage my face and neck when I get very tired. She sometimes appears as a very bright light outside my room. When I asked her why she never appears in the form we all know her, she said, 'I am none of the things of the flesh. You see me only with your heart, which has no form.'

"She tells of events that will affect the consciousness of man. These events will be dramatic ways of communicating and will bring those who remain after the 'cleansing' into closer contact with the needs of the planet."

S.B., psychic counselor, Florida: "Figures in lavender robes and hoods with gentle, kind eyes appeared to me when I was five. They told me that I was special and that they would always be nearby if I needed them.

"Once when I was looking up at the sky, the figures appeared and told me that I had a home there. They also told me that I had special gifts which I would soon learn to use. As an adult, I have had many experiences with spirits of the deceased. The same lavender figures appear regularly, especially when I am troubled. They recently told me that I will be able to return 'home' soon."

P.B., psychiatrist, Pennsylvania: "When I was about five, I was playing inside when I heard a voice tell me to go out into the yard. Someone special wanted to see me. I obeyed and, standing there in the garden, I perceived who, at that time, I believed to be Jesus. This beautifully robed entity told me that I was here on Earth to perform a very special work of helping people. I was told that I would be guided throughout my life."

H.L.L., California: "At age five, I met the entity who became my guide. At the time, I thought she was a real, physical person. But she glided, rather than walked, then disappeared. She scolded me for playing in the mud on a cold day. I had heard her in my head even before that.

"At around the age of eleven, I saw a vision of Jesus. I realized later that it was actually a guide who appeared to me as Jesus, because at that time I was very religious in an orthodox sense and would only accept a guide in that form. The entity used big words which I could not understand at that time, but I remembered them until I could. The gist of what he said was that I was to grow to become aware of all things."

L.P., teacher and counselor, Florida: "When I was five, I packed my little suitcase several times, because I wanted to go to my real 'home.' I began to see what I thought were gnomes. When I lay in bed awake at night, a greenish glow would come to me. It talked to me and comforted me a lot.

"When I was eleven, my 'real' father began to visit me. He was tall and dressed in silver robes. I could never quite see his face, but he had a marvelous, ringing voice. He told me that he would come to take me home when my mission was completed. He told me that I had brothers and sisters that I had not yet met. He called me by the name of 'Leah,' which I adopted, even though my friends shortened the name to 'Lee.' "

Dr. R.L.S., Professor of Education and Psychology, Wyoming: "At five or six, I 'felt' a pull toward another world, as if I had a mission to accomplish here before I could rejoin my 'true home.' I was sad and apprehensive in my task.

"At eleven or twelve, I sensed some spiritual reassurance that I could improve my work as a school pupil. I had a vision of traveling through space.

"At fourteen or fifteen, I experienced a religious 'rebirth' at a church camp. I felt, again, as if I had an important mission in life. Now, I meditate regularly."

During one of Francie's channelling sessions, I asked

why so many of the Star People had their activating vision at around the age of five. Francie communicated the following to me:

"In most cases a Star Person's own glands trigger a genetic memory that was seeded long ago. The DNA packet projects a scenario that totally involves the so-called 'mind's eye' of the young Star Person. It is as if a motion picture filmed long ago is somehow unfolded and played to its end. The activating vision captivates the viewer and affects all thoughts thereafter.

"If you will notice, in so many instances the entities who were seen (projected) were clothed in robes and used a mildly antiquated form of speaking. The 'knowing' that accompanies such visions 'hums' to the very core of one's being, for it speaks of a wisdom that had been embedded in the genetic lineage for generations before the Star Child came to be born.

"In those instances wherein the young Star Person sees angels, the DNA packet has also included within it the awareness that such entities are messengers and great Beings of Light. Some see them on many occasions as powerful beings. Others see but the light source. But the presence of an angel alerts the Star Person to be receptive for a spiritual teaching.

"Those Star People who have seen smallish men—who, while different from humankind, are obviously humanoid—have observed entities from yet another place of origin. In these times of great Earth Changes, this planet is being observed by wise beings who have visited Earth for centuries. They know of the coming cataclysms, though they do not know precisely when they will occur. They are studying how they might interact and aid us when they transpire. Sensitive people, such as the Star People, can sense their presence and have seen these visitors frequently.

"There is never a loss of contact. If one is a Star Person and has received an activating vision, that event has triggered a particular vibration to resonate within them. From that moment on, they begin to affect their surroundings and all those with whom they come into contact, whether they are consciously aware of this or not.

"Different Star People have different roles which they will enact throughout their lives and during the times of great cataclysms. Certain of them will be frequently reactivated at unusual times, but most Star People will be retriggered when in the vibrational 'aura' of another Star Person. They will also be stimulated when perceiving a motion picture, a book, a work of music, an art form, a play, and so forth, that has been produced or inspired by another Star Person. Many Star People are now actively seeking to raise the vibrational patterns of the masses by their creative works, so as to elevate more speedily their awareness.

"A consciously aware Star Person must continuously attempt to elevate himself or herself spiritually and to give of the love vibration so that an open channel to Higher Intelligence may be maintained. A consciously aware Star Person must always aid others to achieve a higher understanding, so as to permit others to see their path to the Source more clearly. For a Star Person is a light bearer and must always attempt to enlighten those whom he or she touches."

Chapter Seven: Trauma at Age Eleven

At about the age of eleven, a large number of the Star People suffered a traumatic experience which caused them to turn inward. In many instances, they became so traumatized that they withdrew from contact with their peers or their families and isolated themselves—if not physically, then emotionally—for a period of time.

Some Star People barely survived accidents or serious diseases during this age sequence of their lives. Others endured rape, beatings, molestations, or persecution. Still others were disturbed by the divorce of their parents, the death of a loved one, or a sudden move which separated them from the security of established friendships and thrust them into new and difficult environments.

Whatever the event, situation, or circumstances, the episode at around the age of eleven somehow served to accentuate the visitation about the age of five. Both experiences appear to have been controlled activating mechanisms for the Star People.

At age five, Marcella R. of Livonia, Michigan, had a vision in which she perceived Time as having no relevance to God. All Time was, somehow, an eternal Now.

Then, at age eleven:

"I nearly died from a massive ear infection. My doctor gave up after two weeks of treatment and turned me over to a specialist on Easter Sunday. I underwent surgery and experienced unbearable pain. Because of this, I became much more aware of the pain suffered by others, and I learned to respect all life—animals and insects, as well as people."

Marcella also gained a firmer linkup with her guardian angel. "My angel communicates when I call upon it. My angel answers questions and dilemmas. If I am in danger, I will hear a warning. Then, in a few minutes, I learn what the danger was. This entity is faceless and androgynous and appears primarily as a light form."

When she was eleven, Mildred B. of Green Valley, Arizona, had an out-of-body experience that was so impressive it left her without further doubt that "one does exist and does have a personality-intelligence apart from the physical body." This assurance "steadied" her into her teens, when she had another out-of-body experience and began a direct voice contact that remained a part of her life from that time onward.

The types of messages she receives, Mildred states, vary greatly: "There is guidance and warnings of danger. There is advice relating to healing. There is assistance with mortal problems. The most wonderful messages are those which contain teachings of spiritual-cosmic truths.

"Lately, messages have been concerned with Earth people and Earth problems during the forthcoming transitional period. The messages relate to the difficult times ahead, with encouragement that 'Now is the time to come forth.' There is a tone of urgency, and it has been indicated that my personal role will become more clarified."

Mildred described the entities which impart these messages to her in the following way:

"Some appear as white lights, others as softly glowing golden lights. Some as figures dressed in white, monk-like robes. Others appear as super mortals, beautiful of face and form. These super mortals are tall, slender, graceful, and perfectly proportioned. They are fair in hair and skin coloring, with a slight, golden tint, akin to a light sun tan. Their green or gray eyes are somewhat almond-shaped, slightly tilted, and set over rather high cheekbones. They are most beautiful."

As I discussed in an earlier book, I had a violent farm accident at the age of eleven and had an out-of-body experience at the time of pseudo-death.

The blades of the farm implement tore at my head, and my world became the color of blood. Suddenly I was floating high above the ground, looking down at the tractor that my seven-year-old sister had somehow managed to bring under control. I was becoming strangely detached from the scene below me. I seemed to be an orangish-colored ball, intent on soaring to the sun. I felt a blissful euphoria, a marvelous sense of Oneness with All That Is. I was scarcely concerned at all with the mangled and dying boy now being carried by my father.

I could be anywhere that I wished, instantly. I thought of my mother—and I was beside her as she labored in the kitchen. I thought of friends—and one by one, I found myself beside them. I seemed to be at one with Time and Space. I did not really care to return to that battered and bloody body where all the pain was.

The nearest hospital in Iowa that could cope with such a terrible accident was in Des Moines, about 140 miles away. I was in and out of the body during that incredible automobile and ambulance drive. And it wasn't until the surgical procedure had begun that some energy seemed to insist that my Essential Self return to the body to cooperate in saving its life.

I remember that I came back with such force that I sat up, shouted, and knocked an intern off-balance. It took the calming words of a Roman Catholic sister to pacify me and to convince me to stop struggling and permit the anesthesia to take affect.

As I consider my own activating episode with the smallish man outside of the kitchen window at age five and the traumatic pseudo-death experience at age eleven, I regard myself as very fortunate. I do not believe that I am special or chosen, but I do feel that an Intelligence outside of myself somehow selected me for the presentation of a certain gift of awareness.

It seems to me that every thinking man and woman eventually asks three very irritating, even haunting, philosophical questions:

Why am I here on Earth?
Will I survive physical death?
Are we, mankind, alone in the universe?

By the time I was eleven, I had had all three of the eternal questions answered for me.

To my satisfaction, in my personal reality, I had discovered that there is an imperishable *something*—the Soul, the spirit, the psyche, call it what you like—within me, within each of us.

The presence of the elf-like humanoid, with his conspiratorial smile, told me that man is not alone, that other intelligences share this turf with us.

And, in my cosmology, I am here because I have a mission to perform. I must inform others of the greater reality which I have perceived. At the same time, I am learning and growing from my struggles and disappointments as I carry out my quest.

Robin R. of Las Vegas, Nevada, experienced a vision of a woman at about the age of twelve that "opened up a whole, new belief system to me."

The entity spoke to Robin, but she feels that the essence of the message remains only in her unconscious at this time. Other humanoid guides have since become available through mental contact. They deliver information to her that is both personal and philosophical.

* * *

At age eleven, Betty B. of Greenwood, Mississippi, had just become aware that others saw her as an "outsider," when she was stricken with scarlet fever. She was unconscious for long periods of time, and during these lapses of consciousness, she left her body and *soared* to other dimensions of reality.

Clyde S. of Phoenix, Arizona, was "visited" at the age of eleven just as he was on the verge of coming down with polio.

"That was before the serum had been invented, but the entity came and stood over me, and I had no paralysis and no aftereffects at all. I could not see the entity, but I heard its footsteps coming and going, and I 'felt' its presence. Nobody in the family had come in to see me during those times, as I learned when I later questioned them."

After this significant visitation, Clyde developed an interest in psychic phenomena, which has now progressed to a desire to explore other dimensions.

"I have highly evolved dreams in which there is always a figure, either a man or a woman, clothed in white standing nearby. Lately, during meditation, I've consciously come into contact with a man in a white robe, who has taken me past the boundaries of our universe and into the presence of a Supreme Being, whom I cannot describe. Although there was no spoken word, it was as if I had been given new duties."

Mark T. Hurst, a poet and an editor with major publishing houses, related that, at the age of five, he saw what he believed to be the face of "God" above billowing clouds.

Today, Mark considers that the face resembled very much a countenance of angelic intelligence. The entity presented no message, but the activating "mind picture" is still very much in his consciousness.

At the age of eleven, Mark contracted rheumatic

fever, which left him with rheumatoid arthritis in his left leg. Although the malady was later cured by cortisone shots, the forced period of inactivity directed him into reading and other introspective activities, rather than sports and more overt physical programs.

Today, Mark retains contact with no specific entity, but his dreams are very often precognitive, and they often feature scenes in which he is flying and floating, free of any mechanical conveyance.

What, I queried during a channelling session with Francie, is the significance of the traumatic experience which occurs in the life experience of so many Star People around the age of eleven?

"Vibrationally, the traumatic event occurs to the Star Person so that he or she will pull inward and go within at that time," Francie related.

"This is a positive thing. The Star Person will learn to seek guidance within his or her own being. This encourages the alpha state of consciousness which aids in triggering various mental mechanisms which slumber within their chromosomal, genetic heritage. This process releases visions, memories, teachings, and attitudinal awareness—all of which were seeded within them.

"Nearly all Star People emerge from the traumatic experience with a renewed sense of purpose. They wish now to live their lives for the betterment of all and, ultimately, for the Source. Each triggering mechanism raises the vibrations of the Star Person to a higher level, with more manifestation of electromagnetic energy.

"All things, even unpleasant, traumatic experiences, occur for the eventual betterment of all humankind for the gaining of awareness, and for the maintaining of contact with the Divine Plan."

Chapter Eight: Beings from Hyperspace and Hypertime

Dr. Roger W. Wescott, Professor and Chairman of the Anthropology Department, Drew University, has commented that one way to cope intellectually with accounts of UFO occupants and other entities is to consider them nothing more than mythical beings.

Such an explanation of the widespread belief in the reality of nonhuman, but humanoid, beings is undeniably reductionistic, Dr. Wescott admits. If one were to frame an explanatory hypothesis that enlarges reality, rather than constricts it, one may be forced into rethinking the nature of the universe in which he lives.

One such way of rethinking things, Dr. Wescott states in his paper, "Toward an Extraterrestrial Anthropology," is to assume that the "real" universe has either more than the three dimensions of space which we perceive or a different type of time-flow from the one we conventionally postulate.

"Time," Dr. Wescott states, "as Western Man has conceived it at least since the Renaissance Period, is single in dimension, uniform in pace, and irreversible in direction. If time should turn out to have more than one dimension, discontinuity of pace, or reversibility of direction, or if space should turn out to have more than three dimensions, then it would be quite possible for solidly and prosaically material beings from the 'real' world to pass through our illusively constricted space-time continuum as a needle passes through a piece of cloth.''

If such interdimensional traffic should exist, Dr. Wescott remarks, we might consider such beings as fantastic ''because they seem to us inexplicably to materialize and vanish.'' We might dismiss them from our reality as hallucinations or hoaxes.

''Rather than existing in space and/or time in the conventional sense of these terms,'' Dr. Wescott offers as an alternative, ''our planet may exist in 'hyperspace' and/or 'hypertime,' where hyperspace is understood to mean space with four or more dimensions and hypertime to mean time which permits events and processes to occur in other than an irreversible linear and unidirectional manner. On such a 'hyperhistorical' sphere or, alternatively, such a historical 'hypersphere,' all the supernatural beings and all the miraculous occurrences known to us from religion and folklore would become explicable as intrusions from the larger earth of reality into the smaller earth of our self-habituation.''

Star People, it would seem, not only perceive beings from ''hyperhistorical'' spheres, they, themselves, on occasion, travel through these hyperspheres.

Rev. Judith Parker of California identified with nearly every item on the pattern profile, then went on to declare that she had the ability to go out of her body and to travel to ''many different dimensions into other galaxies—with or without 'outer space beings.' ''

According to Rev. Parker:

''I belong to a small group of highly evolved people who are constantly traveling into the unlimited dimensions to do very unique psychic surgeries and healings on the spiritual bodies of our patrons, who come to our Aware Center for spiritual enlightenment.

"We have been given previews of very, very futuristic inventions which come to us from other dimensions of life forces far advanced—far beyond Earth's comprehension. Since I was a very small child, I have been shown mental pictures of other worlds. I always felt as though I wanted to get off the world and return to my Space Brothers and Sisters—and my home planet."

Gael Steele of New York claims communication with her "real father and his people" since she was eight years old.

Ten years ago, Gael had a "life-death-life" experience during which she was permitted to return to life with the stipulation that she find others like herself who needed help. Once she had located other Star Children, Gael was to train them in a manner which would be shown to her. According to her report, she now has a group of about twenty.

"The direction and subsequent proofs came from an ancestor of my human father named Lugh Lamphada, 'The Torch,' of the ancient Tuatha de Danann of Ireland, who directs me now to write to you," Gael said. "You seem to have been recognized as some sort of census director for our people."

This is the message which Gael relayed to us:

The Starlords each are repeatedly broadcasting by mindtouch their own introductory message to their children. Some of the children will receive the messages; some have been damaged by restrictions; but to those who will simply "listen" as if someone were about to answer them, perhaps the message will come through.

We are near a time when there will be cataclysms and upheaval on Earth. The Starlords now concerned will pass from our sphere before the time of change. They are attempting to reach any of their children, each with his own message, to inform the children that they may help. But if the whole knowledge of how to help escapes those the Starlords themselves cannot reach, they will miss receiving the information which will help them endure and aid others. Simply foreseeing the Golden Age of Peace, which should come, will not assure the Star Children's being useful until that age arrives. The difficult times have come. Listen! And do not distort by one iota that which *you* hear from the Starlords."

At about the age of eleven, Sheri K. from Kansas City, Missouri, went into a four-week comatose state as a result of an injection of antibiotic. She knows now that she received a great deal of contact with multidimensional beings during her time in that unconscious state, but she is also aware that whatever occurred to her took place on "some realm other than the physical."

Since 1966, she established a rapport with an entity through a state of meditation. In the company of this being, she is able to leave her body and to visit places around the planet. "On one occasion", she writes, "the visit was to another solar system with a blue-white sun.

"The messages I receive are both of information about myself and of guidance and direction in my work (I am an astrologer and a counselor). The entity appears, through my eyes, to be of human form. However, I do not know if my conscious self would allow a 'foreign' image."

When she was a teenager, LaVere Pisut of Florida received a manifestation of an entity who declared himself to be her true father. LaVere was joined in marriage to a fellow Star Person, and the happy products of their union have been a number of Star Children who travel freely through hyperspace and hypertime.

Fourteen-year-old Robin Pisut has astral-projected since babyhood. Animals are attracted to her, and people have sought her out for advice for years now.

When she was five, Robin encountered a "boy" with white-blond hair who taught her strange songs and peculiar words.

A "lady" with long hair also visited Robin often. The

lady took her out-of-body and showed Robin a number of UFOs and their inhabitants. At age eleven, Robin went into a three-hour trance and spoke with her deceased grandmother.

Marc, who is ten years old, was visited at age five by an entity he called the "Old Man." Marc often projects to UFOs. Entities appear to him as colored "dots," and they help him accomplish healings.

Marc often sees a man in a monk's robe, who materializes engulfed in a greenish glow.

During his out-of-body experiences, Marc has traveled to "another universe" and has seen a reddish planet with green craters.

Jason, who is only six years old, was healed of spinal meningitis when he was but three months old. Deafness left him when he was six.

Jason regularly has out-of-body experiences. He has seen UFOs, and the "friends" he sees and to whom he speaks at night often take him "flying."

Elsewhere in this book, Francie has described how multidimensional beings take her out of the body and transport her to an "inbetween universe" so that she might be presented with living diagrams and receive teachings.

As Dr. Roger Wescott has suggested, it may well be time for our materialistic culture to "rethink" the nature of the real universe. Our planet may, indeed, exist in hyperspace and hypertime.

Throughout history, men and women with Star People proclivities have discovered—or have been guided to understand—that Time and Space have many dimensions. And it is in these hyperhistorical spheres that the multidimensional beings originate.

Such an entity who has appeared to me on numerous occasions—both in dreams and in spontaneous, physical manifestations—is named Holeah. She appears nearly always in a Grecian-style robe, trimmed in gold. In physical appearance, she greatly resembles

Francie, only Holeah is considerably taller and always wears her hair curled and piled atop her head. I believe that Holeah's image definitely acted as a triggering mechanism when I first met Francie.

When I have been alerted to dangerous situations, the voice of alarm has often been Holeah's.

When I hear a guiding voice as I work at my typewriter, it comes often in Holeah's soft, feminine tones.

When I have been in need of comforting, it has frequently been Holeah's motherly vibration which has soothed me.

In addition to the manifestation of Holeah on a regular basis, I have been able to encounter my Master Teacher through a meditative technique which Francie has channelled through Kihief. Although it was quite likely my Master Teacher who appeared spontaneously to me to relay the information and instructional materials which I was to share in *Revelation: The Divine Fire*, the process, which Francie calls "The Three Steps to Awareness," has brought me into a closer relationship with this spiritual tutor.

We will be sharing certain details of that meditative technique later in this book, but permit me here to share a teaching which I received in the Golden Temple of Love, Wisdom, and Knowledge.

In an altered state of consciousness, I beheld beautiful gardens surrounding the Golden Temple. The cowled figure holding open his arms in greeting and welcome seemed to be of a sturdy physique under his dark robe.

He was just a bit under six feet tall, and he had a well-trimmed beard and mustache. His eyes were a bright blue, seeming even lighter, clearer, set against his dark complexion. His dark hair, what I could see of it straying out from beneath the cowl, had only a few streaks of gray within its slightly coarse texture.

"I have known you since before you were you," the

teacher said to me, laughing softly. "I was not far away when a master appeared to your mother as a young girl. Do you have knowledge of this event?"

I had such knowledge. My mother had often told me of the time when a robed master had appeared before her sister and herself as they walked on a country road. The entity had materialized with such solidity that his sandals had left clear imprints in the soft gravel as evidence for those who might doubt their testimony.

"We watch carefully over our seedlings," the Master Teacher smiled. "Now," he bade me, "come along to class. The others have already assembled."

"Will *you* teach me"? I asked hopefully.

"Another time," he told me. "An Ancient Holy One speaks tonight."

We entered the beautiful temple of Love, Wisdom, and Knowledge. At the right of the entrance was a remarkable tapestry of superb workmanship.

"Behold the intricate blending of thread and skillful energy," the Master Teacher instructed me.

"This lovely tapestry is here to remind each student that he or she is like an individual thread that runs through the great fabric of life. Although you are but one single thread, you are still important to the entire tapestry. Your thin, interwoven contribution is meaningful to the whole. If you should remove yourself from the great tapestry of life, you will fall to the floor as an inconsequential wisp of thread. You are important and meaningful only as a part of the whole, of the One."

We passed an awe-inspiring golden altar, bedecked with a remarkable array of hundreds of flickering candles.

"Which of the candles give the most light?" my Master Teacher asked. "Which of the candles are the most important?"

"All of the candles give the light," I answered.

"Then none of the candles are important?"

"There is only one light," I responded, "but there are many candles. Each candle is important, for it has a piece of the light. But if a candle should burn out, the light would still continue.

"So it is with humankind," I continued. "There is but one life, one principal Soul energy, and each of us has a piece of Life and Soul."

The Teacher smiled, and placed an approving hand on my shoulder. "That was your lesson three nights ago. I'm happy to learn that you were paying attention."

He ushered me into a large hall where numerous other students had already taken their positions at desks or prayer benches. As it has always been, I could distinguish clearly a few of the faces of my fellow students. As before, the face of the principal Teacher was hidden by a cowl.

Certain facets of this multidimensional world seem always to be hidden from me. When I return to full consciousness in our three-dimensional world, I often have only a dim memory of the essence of the teachings which were imparted. But it is as I sit at the typewriter that the concepts reform and the words recollect themselves.

Robert Gray of Mississippi was one of the first Star People to work with *The Starbirth Odyssey* album when we committed the altered-state techniques to tape cassettes. Here are excerpts from his report, dated April 8, 1979:

> For as long as I can remember, there has been a very strong impression in my mind of a certain day when I was a child of about four or five. All I had ever been able to recall, up until now, had been a vivid vision of the northwest sky from a location close to our home.
>
> There was the feeling within me that there had been some kind of interaction with a superior intelligence, but I had never been able to understand just how such a thing could have been or what could have taken place.
>
> I began my probe of my unconscious on March 29th, using the "Three Steps to Awareness" tapes. Here is an

account of the visions and revelations that I received.

March 29—I retired, using Francie's "Three Steps to Awareness" tape to place me into the sleep state. I silently asked for understanding of whatever would be revealed to me.

March 30—Upon awakening, I received very clear impressions of myself as a child around the age of four or five, discovering and admiring with wonder and excitement a white, vibrant, sphere of light, which seems to be of a gaseous substance. There are four entities watching me.

From my understanding now, I perceive that these entities are from a dimension that is of a vibration that is much higher than ours, but not as high as the level of Soul vibration. They are explaining to me that their place of origin exists in a dimension somewhere between our vibration and Soul vibration. They tell me there is a reason for this.

The strong, dominant figure is a man about seven feet tall. He has a full beard, and his hair is very curly and wavy. The other entities remain in the background, and I can't tell much about them. Due to their rate of vibration, they appear as white in color, with very subtle tracings of blue.

The location of this vision is on the northwest side of the house, behind the well house, with the northwest pasture beyond. As a child, this was always my favorite place to play.

March 31—As I retire, I ask to learn more, once again playing the "Three Steps to Awareness" tape.

April 1—Upon awakening, I have a vision of a vehicle from the same vibratory dimension as the entities. This craft is beautiful and constructed to perfection. It is white in color, with more blue than the beings reveal.

April 1—With the tape playing, I retire with the thought that I will learn more.

April 2—As I awaken, I receive a vision of the interdimensional vehicle hovering. A sphere of white light descends from an opening in the bottom center. I marvel at the beauty of the craft, and it seems as though the blue in the vehicle is more pronounced during this appearance.

April 3 and 4—No probings.

April 4—Retire with the tape and the thought of learning more.

April 5—As I awaken, the image of the seven-foot-tall being comes to me. The vision is very strong. It is as if he is one with me, and yet, we are separate.

This time he holds an object that looks like a streak of lightning. It is not large, but medium-sized to small. It appears to be made of gold, yet it is a substance from their vibratory range.

A remarkable living vision of myself as a child trying to play with the ball of light came up around us. I see the entities watching me as they did when I was four or five. I am greatly surprised by the sudden appearance of this vision. The tall entity is watching me with heavy concentration, and he seems to be very pleased.

April 5—I retire with the thought that I will learn more.

April 6—Upon awakening, I see a vision of myself in the future. We are in the midst of a major earthquake. Many people are in shock. I feel alone and I am wondering what to do. The entity—I have come to know him as Mark—appears to me and says, "Know that we are always with you. You are to help these people to restore order."

I see myself in a cave with other Star People. We are working with a people from another world who are operating through us to help the inhabitants of Earth. These entities are bringing supplies to us in a dark, gray vehicle. The Earth people depend upon us greatly, and we must use our psychic abilities very strongly.

April 7 and 8—No visions. The thought occurs to me that, for the time being, this should be the end of my mind probe.

I would like to say that I have never experienced anything like this on the psychic level. The visions which I received, together with associated feelings and thoughts, had greater impact than reality at both the objective and subjective levels of my psyche. This was a *total* experience.

There were other thoughts, visions, and feelings which I received while working with the cassettes, but to tell everything would take too much time and too much writing.

Joan Sotkin contacted us to state how it was her communication with Beings of Light which guided her to establish the Health Corps and the Inner Ecology system in Los Angeles.

Joan had been suffering from severe depression and a wide variety of physical disorders, including colitis, gastritis, sinusitis, anemia, insomnia, bronchitis, and circulatory problems. In 1973 she was diagnosed as a hypoglycemic and found her way at last to a nutritionist/endocrinologist who helped her on the path to restored health.

Joan was told that a lifetime as a sugar junkie and thirty years of prescription drugs had taken their toll on her body. She had severe adrenal exhaustion, vitamin and mineral deficiencies, enzyme disorders, and liver dysfunction.

It was while she was undergoing various detoxification processes that she began to spend many hours in meditation. In December of 1975, the "voices" came to her to offer guidance in establishing the Health Corps. Since that time, Joan has received over a thousand pages of channelled material from the Beings of Light.

"The actual purpose of the Health Corps is to help the people of the planet clear their body-mind vehicles in order to allow the higher energies to come through," Joan told us. "We teach people how to accomplish the clearing carefully so that there is a minimum of discomfort. The result of the process is elimination of physical and mental disorders."

Harold F. of Seattle, Washington, commented that he was delighted that the Star People are "coming out into the open."

In Harold's opinion: "Without doubt, individuals throughout the country are discovering a new meaning for their lives. Too many persons have had experiences of a similar nature for the whole situation to be a coincidence."

Harold went on to say that he had had numerous

meetings with "spiritually advanced beings." In his personal assessment of his experiences, they had been accompanied by a "very high degree of spirituality" and were "quite positive and uplifting."

Illiana, who channels the publication *New Age Teachings* in Brookfield, Massachusetts, provided us with these insights about her development as a sensitive and her interaction with Light Beings:

"At approximately the age of five, I began to have what my parents termed 'imaginary friends.' I did not 'see' these friends in the usual way, but I did *experience* them.

"At about the age of twelve and a half, I received an *inner* experience. At this time, my parents and I were attending some religious lectures. We had been Roman Catholics and we were now considering some changes.

"One night, following a very fine lecture, I came out of the auditorium feeling so good, so different from any other time. Perhaps to say that an Inner Being had entered my body and had poured Light Beams in every cell of my body would give some idea of the 'feeling' I had. I felt warm, loving, totally delightful, and *free*. I was literally walking on air.

"The same thing had happened to my father. In fact, it was he who had first spoke of how he felt. We were both so exhilarated. From that day forward, Dad was able to read, something he could not do prior to this experience, because he had been deprived of an education.

"As for myself, until that time I had had a monotone singing voice. I could not carry a tune. From that night onward, I had a singing gift bestowed upon me that I have used ever since to provide Consciousness Raising Music. Also, from that night onward, I dedicated my life to working for God. There is no doubt that this experience provided me with my awakening as to who I really am.

"Until fourteen years ago, my contact with the Realm

of Light had been on an orthodox religious path. I also studied various doctrines and dogmas, from Catholicism to the Eastern religions. I realize that this was a necessary and an important learning so that I might be empathetic with the religious struggles of others.

"Then, fourteen years ago, I 'heard' through telepathic communication the first messages given directly to me. Since that time, I always receive contact from the Messengers of Light through a telepathic 'sensing' of the messages. Then, after a period of deep silence and meditation, I write the impressions down on paper.

"The messages are always of a high spiritual nature. Never do I receive the kind of 'psychic' impressions which others do, nor do I seek them. I prefer to be a Channel of Light, on the Truths which must be revealed to humankind in these changing times."

Seeking to acquire more knowledge about the beings from "hyperspace" and "hypertime," I asked Francie the following questions while she was channelling:

How do the multidimensional beings move through time and space?

"One method is by thought. They can *think* and then reassemble their energy at another given thought-location.

"On occasion, they send an image of themselves to a receiver through this process. They may alter the image of themselves to suit the belief construct of the receiver, but the image is so profound that the entity appears to be there in the physical.

"Another way the beings travel from one dimension to another is by lowering their vibratory rate for a short period of time. This method is somewhat dangerous for them, however, for to stay at a lower vibration for a length of time might possibly entrap them in that dimension.

"The beings also travel by a process that shall be known to us in a relatively short period of time.

"There exists within the Starseed's chromosomal

makeup inherent memories, images, characteristics, awarenesses, which were purposely implanted there long ago. When certain vibrations occur, whether triggered by environmental stimuli or glandular discharges, these time-release capsules of awareness and enlightenment go off and project images into the brains of the Starseed.

"There is also a method of interdimensional travel which shall be 'triggered' very soon."

Is the world of Holeah a physical one?

"Holeah exists today in a dimension of a vibratory rate higher than our own.

"Holeah is one of those extraterrestrials who came to Earth many centuries ago. She and her kind were from a planet that was rapidly evolving upward in frequency rate. Even as they came to Earth, their home planet was in the process of becoming pure energy and returning to the Source of All That Is.

"Holeah and her kind were both brilliant and compassionate. They knew that their physical bodies were also in the process of acceleration to a higher level of vibration. In order to perpetuate knowledge of their world and in order to accelerate humankind's spiritual elevation, as well as their own, they caused essences from their very beings to exist within the bodies of the human life forms they found on this planet. Within the seed inherited from Holeah and her people are memories of their past, which shall become our future. This was a loving act on the part of the extraterrestrials.

"The world that Holeah shows you in visions is the world that she once knew on her home planet. You walk together in her memories, but she teaches you of your own future."

Where is the Golden Temple, of which so many Star People speak, actually located?

"There is a vibration between physical Earth and the level which is now occupied by the elevated extraterrestrials, the Sowers, who have continued their upward evolution. This is a place designed for learning to which we can ascend with an aspect of our multidimensional selves. So-called 'classes' there accelerate the student's development.''

When does one graduate from this school?

''Graduation is as it is on the physical level. When one has embraced and learned all there is to gain at that level, he graduates in vibrational frequency.

''Graduation is an automatic energy process— painless, beautiful, and destined.''

Has Kihief ever lived on Earth?

''Kihief himself has never lived on Earth, but I was told that an essence from his being was caused by him to exist here—seeded, if you will.''

Is he truly what we would consider an angel in the biblical sense of that term?

''Yes, a beautiful, glowing being, who could appear and disappear at will, bearing a spiritual message, is called an angel. Throughout history many extraterrestrials have appeared to Earthlings as angels, because they lowered their vibratory rate so that they might more fully interact with humankind.

''Even when the extraterrestrials first came to Earth, their appearance was more attractive, more godlike, more glowing, than our lesser and more animal expression of the Life Force. They had already begun to show evidence of their increased vibratory rate, and they not only possessed great mental powers, but an incredible technology, as well.''

Chapter Nine: The UFO Factor

Like so many Star People, Suzanne M. of North Carolina has had many dreams of UFOs. When she was five, she remembers having a frequent dream of something looking down at her from the sky. The white, oval light fixture on the ceiling used to cause her discomfort.

Around the age of eleven, she dreamed repeatedly of UFOs landing out in their yard. In her waking state, she used to fantasize about traveling to a twin Earth.

When she read the initial *National Enquirer* article about the Star People, Suzanne felt her spine "tingle," because two years prior to her learning of our research, she had written the following while in an altered state of consciousness:

"There are certain people on Earth who have descended from the stars. They are on a mission to help stranded souls who have become confused. These people are different from other people in that they seem to dazzle with a stronger output of energy. Indeed, if their energy could be measured, it would be stronger than many, regular auras. But psychic sensitives can perceive it and know the powerful Star People who spin fire in their vortex during the changing of planes.''

On June 14, 1979, according to Suzanne, she experienced the first of a chain of events "which would change my entire life."

At approximately 7:45 P.M., she saw an oval-shaped, silver disk fly over her yard, ascend into the clouds at a sharp right angle, then circle back.

Exactly two weeks later, June 28 at approximately 7:55 P.M., as she was walking home through an old cemetery, she felt a "cool flow through the top of my head."

When she looked up, Suzanne was fascinated to see a glowing, oblong object overhead. She felt a strong desire to communicate with "them," and she believed that she could somehow achieve her goal.

"I saw them many more times in the same spot, until about the time of the autumn equinox. During this time, all sorts of messages and symbols flowed through my mind. I believe that I was definitely in telepathic contact with extraterrestrials."

Suzanne's inner guidance told her that a part of her is linked to the UFOnauts, but her Soul, "in order to grow, has had to suffer with the Earth people."

Here are certain messages which Suzanne shared with us from her series of contact experiences:

"Often an advanced member of another planetary system is sent on a mission. He is programmed to forget so that he can gain experiences the Earth way, then gradually awaken to the realization of what he really is. He is guided to accomplish certain things, primarily the enlightenment of the ones who are ready."

"The physical form is an exact replica of the energy form which created it."

*   *   *

"Life on one plane and evolutionary system is not attuned to life on other levels of existence, because the vibratory rate of the substance composing its beings is different."

"At this time in evolution, we are, indeed, in the development of a Sixth Kingdom, a new species, exceeding humankind. Eventually, the Soul goes on to even higher things, such as developing new Hierarchical archetypes of planetary systems. Even after graduating from that level, there are still many, many higher levels and authorities."

"All emanate from a common Source. All is energy and vibration. Solar radiation consists of vibratory long-wave energies, as well as short-wave finger energies. The self-consciousness, or ego, breaks away and flows into the stream of universal consciousness. Light and sound is within all."

Dale Iodice of Massachusetts, remembers hearing a voice saying, "I am your father," when she was five years old. She associated the voice with a UFO.

When she was eleven, she heard the voice again, repeating that it came from her "father." At this time she actually observed UFOs, and one of the sightings was also witnessed by a neighbor.

"I begged my father to take me back to the mother ship," Dale said, "but the voice only repeated, 'I am your father.'

"During another sighting, when I asked to be taken aboard, the voice said, 'We only took the children who weren't wanted.' "

Dale has told us that her contact with her "father" is now firmly established.

"I hear him in meditations, sometimes in dreams. Other times, there is a feeling in my mind. When he wishes to speak, I know. Abstinence from heavy foods helps. He reassures me of my mission to help people who are unaware of the changes to come. I am to establish an arc of energy and remain a beacon light for others.

"One time he appeared to me in a Christ-like image," Dale stated. "But now he appears hairless, a flame glowing where the third eye would be. He is quite tall and wears a robe wrapped around him. He wears a necklace of blue and white crystals."

Kathi W. of St. Louis Park, Minnesota, was not yet three years old when her initial contact with UFO intelligences occurred. She recalls that she was sitting on the living room floor of their farmhouse, playing in the sunlight. She fell into a kind of sleep, and two beings appeared and talked to her.

"I don't remember what they said to me," Kathi noted, "but they told me that when I woke up, I was to look at my left leg. They had left something by which to remember their visit.

"When I awakened, I looked at my leg and found a mark on my upper left thigh. I remember trying to erase it and rub it off, but it was like a birthmark. I know that it hadn't been there before.

"I remembered this experience recently, when I first read about the Star People. I told my boyfriend about it, and he pointed out to me that the mark was in the domed, saucer-shape of a UFO."

When Kathi was five, she remembers suddenly feeling extreme alienation and loneliness.

"I was just walking down the street when I thought, 'Who am I?', 'What am I doing here?', 'Where am I?' I went home, but I felt that I did not belong there or with my family. I have felt distinctly misplaced since that day."

Kathi says that she saw her first UFO in 1953, "a

beautiful, glowing, pearlescent globe hanging in the sky, perfectly still, on a windy March day.''

Ed M. of Cabot, Arkansas, referred to the entities that came to him as a child as angels. To prove their corporeal, as well as ethereal, existence, he once asked them to turn on a desk lamp in his room, a lamp with a particularly stiff switch. The light came on.

Ed had awakened inexplicably just a few nights before and had been drawn to look out the window. "I saw a whirling, bright, silver UFO disappearing in the sky," he said.

"In my early childhood," Ed went on, "the messages that I received were that I was not of this Earth. I was told that I had a special mission. Also, I was not of my parents in the same way that other children were of their parents.

"It's still unclear to me, but one of the messages was that the world is a dream, that is, of an insubstantial nature.

"I was informed that I was not who I appeared to be in everyday reality. My 'true' person was different. Because of such messages, I never felt as though I had a true childhood.

"Even before I entered kindergarten, I would, on occasion, insist to my parents that they were not truly my parents. I rationalized that I had been adopted, even though my confused and disturbed parents showed me my birth certificate.

"These messages came to me in dreams and in reverie states from silvery and bright beings," Ed explained. "They seemed quite tall, and they wore whitish or dark blue tunics. Some seemed like patriarchal males with longish hair. The females had a 'Virgin Mary' feeling to them. Their 'bodies' were ethereal."

Since he was a child, Ed has had recurring dreams of himself and others boarding spacecraft. "I can't be sure if these are past-life memories, future visions, or both,'' he revealed.

An unusual account of long term interaction with UFO entities came to us from Johnny K. Johnny had a tragic childhood in which he came to serve as the physical scapegoat for the others in his large family. Whenever anything in their collective lives went wrong, Johnny was beaten in an almost ritualistic manner by both his parents and his three brothers and one sister.

One night, when he was about five years old, his father whipped Johnny into unconsciousness and left him lying on the ground.

"I awoke that night, looking up at the stars", Johnny reported. "We lived out in the country, and we didn't have a yardlight to mask out any stars. I was lying in the grass. It was so soft and cool. I knew that if I got up and went into the house, my brothers would make me sleep under the bed, so I lay there where it was nice and clean.

"I decided that I could not go on living that way, and I prayed to God that he come to take me that night. I was in a lot of pain. I didn't want to wake up in the morning.

"Then seven unusually bright stars caught my eyes. They kept changing places with each other and coming closer. They stopped about twenty feet above the farmhouse. Even though they were glowing and pulsating, they didn't seem to cast any light on the ground.

"I was not frightened. I really thought that it was God coming to get me.

"Seven beings then approached me. They seemed to float across the ground. I could hear no footsteps, and their robes did not stir. When the beings moved, it sounded like static electricity popping. The moon was out, and I could see quite well. They had no facial features. They looked like three-dimensional shadows.

"The beings came to me and formed a circle around me. My pain ceased, and they started putting images in my mind. There were no verbal sounds—only something like a movie in my mind. (This is the way they've been teaching me in all subsequent visits).

"The circle they formed around me has always reminded me of the kind shaped by different tribes when they contact their gods. After they formed the circle, they began to sway from side-to-side and hum—'Mmmmmm, Mmmmmmm.' I felt a tingling sensation all over me. I soon fell asleep. I don't know when they left, but I awakened the next morning with a sense of purpose for my life."

Johnny said that all of his visitations up until the time he entered military service were of a religious, inspirational nature, even though, at that period of his life, he was unchurched and did not read the Bible.

He went on to share a number of UFO-related experiences with us; but perhaps the most significant, in terms of our Star People research, concerned the recurring dream which he first had several years ago on the night when the seven beings formed the circle around his beaten body.

"That night I dreamed that I was standing in front of a great city," Johnny said. "The city was inside a dome of transparent material, and outside of the outer dome, was yet another dome. Looking past the city through the domes were other domes, somehow connected to a huge structure. I saw a man standing in front of the city, which, in later years, I realized was me.

"As I stood there, a woman came up and began to speak to me. Then, all of a sudden, everything began shaking, and the buildings and the domes began to collapse. I grasped the woman's hand and began to run to a place of safety.

"It wasn't until I saw the picture in the *Enquirer* that I realized that woman was you [Francie]. If you hadn't been wearing your hair up, just as you did in the dream, I might not have known for certain that it was you. Too many coincidences have happened for me not to write to you. I started having that dream with you in it over twenty years ago.''

Billie Selph of Florida is one of a number of Star People who are convinced that they have met actual extraterrestrials living here on Earth, apart from the Starseeded members of our own species.

When she was about the age of five, ethereal figures in lavender robes and hoods, with gentle faces and kind eyes, appeared to her. They told Billie that she was ''special,'' that they were truly her family, and that they would always be nearby if she needed them.

It was when she was living near Cape Canaveral many years later that she encountered ''what some would call 'aliens.' ''

Billie had had a number of UFO sightings in the area and a few days before Apollo 11 was to be launched, a stranger came into the place where she worked.

''He wouldn't talk to anyone but me, and nobody knew him,'' Billie recounted. ''This man knew things about me that *nobody* else knew. He said that I had been watching his ship at nights. He told me that Apollo 11 should not follow the course that had been set for it. 'They' were trying to help so that certain dangerous mistakes would not be made. The night before Apollo 11 was launched, he said goodbye to me.

''Some years later, when I was working up North, another man came into the place where I worked, and he, too, was a stranger to everyone, and who would only talk to me. He looked just like the man I had met near Cape Canaveral, except he had a goatee. Just like the first man, this one knew things about me that nobody else could know.

''He came into the place where I worked for several nights. He said that he was from one of the UFOs that I had been seeing recently—even though I had never mentioned that I had ever seen any UFOs. He also told me about my 'home,' the purple-misted planet. He said that they were in actual control of Apollo 13.

"Both visitors were tall, with chiseled features, sharp noses, high foreheads, piercing blue eyes. Both of them looked very much like my 'family' in their purple robes."

Valerie B. of Warrenville, Illinois, also believes that she has encountered extraterrestrials in physical form who were aware of her mission as a Star Person.

"When I was five years old, I could hear a woman's voice—not my physical mother's—which talked to me whenever I was in any kind of danger. I have always been a telepath and an empath.

"At the age of seven, I wrote a book about a spaceship coming to take me home. I discovered at the age of nine that I could travel along the time track outside of my body."

Valerie has seen UFOs on eleven occasions. Once when she was a student at Northern Illinois University, she saw a cigar-shaped craft "in broad daylight in a blue, cloudless sky."

"When I was working as an editorial assistant, I was given some photographs from a science program—I was editing a television guide. One picture was of a microbe, the other was of a galaxy. I went for lunch, taking my work with me.

"A man, who appeared to be in his fifties, came into the restaurant and began to speak to me as if he knew everything about me. It was as though the photos were some kind of code, sign, or symbol. We agreed to meet for lunch the next day. He had a tape in his car that said that he was from another planet that maintained a kind of 'peace corps' here on Earth.

"In 1971, when I went to Houston, I met an inventor who had the same tape and who said that he was working with extraterrestrials. Both of these individuals told me that I wasn't from Earth. They said that, genetically, I was from another galaxy.''

On one occasion, while Francie was channelling, I asked her about UFOnauts.

Are there physical entities from other worlds now observing or visiting Earth?

''Yes, there are physical entities which exist throughout the universe. There are also paraphysical entities, who are more or less physical. Some entities of both types do visit or observe Earth in order to study its emanations and its people.

Are any of these entities who are presently observing us the descendants of the extraterrestrials who also seeded the Star People?

''More correctly, some are the *relatives* of those who seeded the Star People. Many of them have a 'starseed' of sorts within them.''

What do these various UFOnauts want with Earth?

''Depending on their level of awareness, they wish to study, to observe, to raise their consciousness. However, they will not directly interfere with our progress, for a direct act of interference with a planet's physical evolution causes a shock which is seen and known to be a direct violation of All That Is.

''The actions of these extraterrestrials must, therefore, be indirect, rather than direct. They must only observe, not interfere. All is vibration. They would impede their own progress if they affected ours negatively. They must never violate the motion of all life, which is returning upward to the Source.

''There is but one major transgression throughout the universe. On this violation hangs all other 'sins': One must never interfere with, nor in any way impede, the motion of another on his or her return to the Source.''

Will the UFOnauts ever physically interact with us?

''They will physically interact with us when we have,

as a species, elevated ourselves in awareness so that we will more naturally blend with their own level of consciousness. We are vibrationally rising now. The birth throes of a new level of awareness is coming to Earth. During the 1980s and 1990s, these birth pangs will affect all the inhabitants of Earth.

"But Earth will then emanate a higher vibration, a finer energy. All physical things on the planet will have evolved and raised its vibrations higher. All physical energy forms will experience a transcendence in vibrational rate. This elevation will begin to come to us in the 1980s and 1990s. Some see this transcendence as destruction, but it is really the birth of a new world."

Chapter Ten: Unusual Birth and Prebirth Experiences of the Star People

LaVere Pisut of Florida told us that she carried three of her four babies to ten-month terms. "They were born awake," LaVere said, "and they could hold their heads up almost immediately. They spoke, read, and counted before most children crawl."

The entire Pisut family has "visitors" who appear often to them, and they have channelled a book of sayings and drawings through automatic writing and artwork.

From childhood, LaVere felt in contact with an alien who told her that she was actually his daughter and that he would one day come to take her home.

"Now, I'm thirty-seven years old," she remarked, "and I still yearn to go home. My children, I find, are also waiting for the same thing."

LaVere and her family, together with ten other Star People, are preparing to build a spiritual retreat in the mountains of Arkansas. She knows of another retreat in Utah, yet another in North Carolina. "Included in these groups are school teachers, police officers, nurses, artists, a publishing agent, an accountant, a former government agent—none of us weirdos or hippies at all.''

Although members of the three groups did not have contact with one another until after the land purchases had been made, LaVere revealed that "when we talked, we found we have one thing in common. Each time we walk outside at night, we look into the stars and say the same thing: 'I am ready.' ''

Anne S.C. of Denver, Colorado, was "filled with joy" to learn that there were others like her.

"When I called my mother and asked her to tell me what she could about me, she told me that the night that I was born she had had an unusual dream," Anne disclosed. "In her dream, she went somewhere and someone showed her all of our family's past female lineage. She saw cubicles all in a row, and in each was to be seen an image (a duplicate or a recorded vibration) of each of the 'grandmothers' who had preceded me.

"Mother knew that she was seeing each of the female ancestors of our line, and she was told that she was viewing them *back to the time that we came to Earth.* Now those were her exact words. I will not change or elaborate upon them.

"My mother is Southern Baptist and very religious. She does not embrace beliefs like mine at all. We have had a gap between us for thirteen years or longer about my feelings. I have always *known* I was different. My eyes cause comment, to say the least. I am always attracting attention, whether I wish to or not. People seem to gravitate to me for some reason.

"When I was about five, someone talked to me with his mind, telepathically. The man who spoke to me mentally came at night in the oak trees near our house. I got spanked for telling Mother and for trying to slip outside to see him.

"When I was eleven, I secretly star-worshipped the old gods, especially Venus. I got up in the early mornings to walk in predawn light to see the Morning Star. I tried to belong to the world, but I knew that I really did not. I withdrew at this time to be by myself, my books, and nature. I was told that I was too old for my age.

"I knew that I had lived before and that I had come from somewhere else to Earth to perform a mission."

Leah Warner of Illinois clearly remembers being "somewhere else" and having someone, perhaps a male elder, show her "pieces" of her life before she was born.

"I sensed my guide was male and that he was an energy form," Leah recalled. "I remember thinking, 'What an opportunity this life will be.' And it has been!

"At the age of twelve, I rebelled against formal religion and standard school systems. I dropped out of public school for two years, and my parents were forced to hire a private tutor for me. I rebelled against, and was not subject to, group mind. I felt like a mutant—and I still do.

"In the past fourteen years—I'm now thirty-eight—I have experienced what others have considered many varied spiritual gifts. I look back on these abilities as a part of a learning process.

"Three years ago, I experienced both a physical and a spiritual transition which lasted for four months.

"During and after this ordeal, an entity made frequent appearances to me and spoke to me. He had sandy blond hair, a beard and mustache. He wore a long, white caftan-type robe, and he emanated unfathomable love. I took him to be Jesus. He spoke in parables, which were sometimes confusing, but, later, would prove to be relevant.

"'I now question whether he wasn't the 'Other' for me. He no longer externalizes for me. We seem to be as one. During the last manifestation, he said he would never leave me and that I was to be comforted by that knowledge. I am!''

"We, as humans, have no control over where or to whom we will be born," Francie has been told. "It is the responsibility of the Soul to see that we are born into the proper environmental circumstances which will aid us to achieve greater awareness and to enrich the level of Soul vibrations toward the Source.

"The Soul seeks to return to the domain of highest vibration occupied by God and other Souls who did not lower their vibrations. Therefore, the Soul selects each facet of life from the viewpoint of which sex, race, parents, country, culture, and environment will afford it with the greatest vibrational patterns of learning.

"We human facets, who go through the various experiences which bring awareness, also learn and become more wise. This causes our spirit within to raise its vibrations when it encounters the higher frequencies of Love, Wisdom, and Knowledge. Our reward for raising our vibrations, for becoming more aware, is to blend as one with the Soul and to ascend to 'Heaven.'

"Upon the parting of our spirit from our physical shell, in what is called death, we can then become incorporated in the higher vibrations of our Soul; and we will, therefore, ultimately return with the Soul when it ascends to the Source.

"For those who are starseeded," Francie continued, "a two-fold process of selection was made by the Soul. First, of course, vibrational patterns were selected for the gaining of the Soul. Second, Starseeds are prodded to be where they will be able to affect the vibrational awarenesses of all those around them. They are placed in positions where they might affect the greatest number of people so that they might aid humankind in its evolution and in its times of greatest need. When a Soul prompts a Starseedling, it is more for the gaining of others than just for the gaining of that Soul's vibrational input."

From Francie's earliest memory, her grandmother figured prominently in her recognition of her own psychic abilities. In retrospect, Francie recognizes her interaction with Martta Barbier as another example of how the starseed may be passed from one generation to another.

"Grandmother Martta had obviously been a very attractive girl in her home town in Italy, but the attention that she received often went far beyond her looks," Francie observed. "Although her conversations and reminiscences sparkled with amusing anecdotes, I knew that there was something in addition to our physical relationship which bound us together.

"I had experienced a number of awesome visions since I had been four and a half," Francie stated. "Although the things that I had seen were far beyond my tender years, Grandma would always listen to the accounts quietly and appear unimpressed.

"She believed me totally, and she would tell me so; but then she would recount an episode from her past that would be presented in such a way as to appear far more unusual than my experience. It seemed as though she could always 'top' whatever had occurred to me.

"This never upset me," Francie clarified, "for her visions had been profound, and many of the manifestations had been observed by several witnesses. She had received widespread recognition for her visions. Her picture had appeared in several important Italian newspapers, and she had once received a reward and a commendation from the King.

"No, being 'topped' by this beloved Grandma never 'smarted,'" Francie pointed out. "Rather, hearing her accounts helped to make me feel more at ease regarding my own visionary experiences. In fact, I considered that my visions weren't very unusual at all, considering that *she* was my grandmother.''

Francie recalled the occasion when she predicted that her dance instructor, a vibrant young woman in her twenties, would soon become critically ill and die. Within a few weeks, the instructor died unexpectedly of cancer.

Grandma Martta listened to the saddened child explaining how she had foreseen the death of a respected instructor, then she told Francie how she had once been sought out by the spirit of a dead woman, who materialized to her and begged her to travel across town to tell the surviving husband where a valuable legacy could be found.

The spirit told Martta that if her husband but raised up their large bed, he would discover a box hidden within its structure. The box would contain two pieces of paper which would bear the signatures of two women to whom she had pawned her golden candlesticks and some jewelry.

The spirit beseeched Martta to make her husband understand that she had died unexpectedly before she had been able to retrieve the valuable objects. The spirit was ashamed that the two business friends had planned to keep their acquisitions a secret from the husband, relying upon her assurance that she was too embarrassed to inform her husband of what she had done.

Martta did as the spirit had bade her. She crossed town, knocked on the man's door, told her vision to the man who incredulously identified himself as the deceased woman's husband. True to the spirit's promise, Martta and the startled man found the box underneath a hidden chamber in the bedboards. The two women were shown the notes and pressured into accepting the husband's money and into returning the valuable gold pieces.

The law enforcement officers, who had accompanied

the husband to each of the two unfaithful friends, corroborated the story of the vision to the newspapers, and Martta's picture accompanied the amazing story. The King, upon learning of the vision that had brought about justice, sent Martta a large envelope, thanking her for her responsible actions and enclosing a monetary reward.

"Grandma had 'topped' me again," Francie laughed. "But hearing her tell this story caused me to feel warm and comforted that I was not really so unusual. This woman, who was my loving grandma, was far more unusual than I, and she had become admired and respected for her gift."

Many years, many personal obligations, and thousands of miles physically separated Francie and her grandmother, until November of 1979, when she was determined to return home for a visit. Francie soon had her grandmother laughing, telling old stories, and even singing in her native tongue. Then Martta suddenly became quiet and said that it was time to tell Francie of several events which she had withheld from her.

"She told me that she had been visited by an angelic being in a flowing white robe on several occasions," Francie said. "This being had repeatedly advised her that I would be born a girl, that my life would have a special mission, that I would know of beings beyond, and that I would be as psychic as she was and her father before her.

"The angel said that I would know of things to come, the way she had always known, and that I would see those on the other side and talk to them, as she had always been able to do throughout her life.

"Grandma was also told of my psychic inheritance by a beautiful woman over six feet tall," Francie continued her account of the visit. "The woman's eyes were large and oddly slanted. The beautiful woman manifested to Grandma on several occasions—many times when she least expected such an encounter.

"Grandma repeated that both the angelic being and the beautiful woman had testified to her of my intuitive abilities, of my destiny, and of my purpose of birth."

Francie admitted that she had sat in awe as Martta related such experiences to her. "I was amazed that, even though we had spent years of endless hours together, she had kept all these things from me."

When Francie asked her grandmother why she had not disclosed such information years before, Martta's only answer was that she had long since learned that the majority of other people do not understand about visions. She was fearful that the rest of the family might get upset with her.

"I decided to wait until you grew up," she said, shrugging off the question.

"But," she added, a merry sparkle in her eye, "I told your father, Joseph, that you were just like me. I told your aunts, Nira Mae and Ann, you were just like me. Your picture is in the papers, just like me. You have the 'power,' just like me, and help people do what's right, just like me. You talk to the Angels just like me."

Martta paused, smiling at Francie in a peculiarly smug way. "But," she asked, "have you ever won any money?"

Francie had to admit that she had not.

"Well," Martta laughed triumphantly, "I have won over two thousand dollars. Fifty dollars from the King. Five hundred through a dream. Six hundred . . ."

Francie joined her grandmother's laughter. Grandma had "topped" her again.

Chapter Eleven: Transcending the Physical Body

Dr. Dale Ironson, assistant professor of psychology at Franklin Pierce College in Rindge, New Hampshire, has suggested that as many as thirty percent of the "normal, healthy population" have had an out-of-body experience (OBE) at least once in their lifetime.

In a study conducted by Dr. Charles Tart at the University of California, forty-four percent of one hundred and fifty students reported having OBEs.

In a similar study carried out by the late Dr. Hornell Hart of Duke University, the figure of those having OBEs was twenty-seven percent.

Dr. Stanley Krippner, a psychologist and a former director of the Maimonides Dream Laboratory in New York, commented that the two studies cited by Dr. Ironson, together with a third conducted by Dr. John Palmer at the University of Virginia, indicate that as many as three out of ten people have had OBEs. This ratio makes it probable that well over sixty million Americans have had out-of-body experiences.

Among Star People, the ratio of those who have OBEs would probably be as high as seven or eight out of ten. And a great number of them claim to be able to experience them at will.

According to my research with OBEs and related phenomena, now based on over twenty years' study and investigation, out-of-body experience appears to be an aspect of mankind's unknown powers that does peculiar things to the conventional concept of a three-dimensional world and the accepted boundaries of the space-time continuum. Although many people regard the notion of projecting one's "astral self" as something springing directly from a science fiction writer's imagination, the phenomenon—like all facets of "psi"—has been noted for centuries.

It seems to me that spontaneous OBEs fit into one of seven general categories:

1. Projection in what appear to be dreams while the subject is sleeping.

2. Projection while the subject is undergoing surgery, childbirth, tooth extraction, and so forth.

3. Projection at the time of accident.

4. Projection during intense pain.

5. Projection during illness or extreme fatigue.

6. Projection during pseudo-death, wherein the subject appears to die for several moments and is subsequently revived and restored to life. It is in this category that many subjects describe their meetings with masters, teachers, and angel guides.

7. Projection at the moment of death, when the deceased subject appears to a living percipient, usually a person with whom he or she has had an emotional link.

There would seem to be an eighth category, but it should be set apart from the spontaneous occurrences, which happen during rather dramatic—and often painful—moments in one's life. *Number Eight* would be conscious out-of-body projections, in which the subject deliberately seeks to catapult his spirit from his physical shell. It is in this category that the Star People would seem to excel.

* * *

In 1967, Betty G. of Nashville, Tennessee, had a "soul-shattering encounter" with a being that appeared in angelic form. This confrontation, according to Betty, completely changed her life.

"I felt so 'filled' with a brilliant, pale, yellow light that I thought I must be glowing like a light bulb," she said. "I was totally saturated with such overwhelming love, that even now I cannot speak of it without crying. From that moment on, I knew that I was never alone, and that I could handle anything that might happen in my life."

Shortly after her remarkable encounter, Betty had her first "wide-awake out-of-body experience." She remembers that she could feel the wind on her face and that she could "see my physical body sitting in my kitchen while 'I' was outside, flying around the neighborhood."

Betty had a pseudo-death experience in 1973, and she was able to watch the doctors frantically working on her physical body while the "real" Betty floated near the ceiling.

"Only three pints of my rare RH-negative blood saved my life," she recalled. "I nearly died twice more in the following four days. The last time, I distinctly heard an authoritative voice *ask* me if I wanted to live or die. I knew that whatever I decided *would* happen, and only a strong urgency to complete what I had started with my writing made me choose life. The voice said, 'So be it,' and the final crisis passed.

"I have since felt that time is running out, and I feel driven by a desperate urgency to finish what I was sent here to do.

"I sense I am a kind of messenger. I have always felt *on*, but not *of*, the Earth.

"Of my most recent three and one-half books, I entirely dreamed the first one, parts of the next two, and most of the one that I am working on now. I feel information is being filtered down to me from another dimension.

"My main character in three books is named Lia. Another, whom I call Lyric, lives in a crystal city and is featured in *Starsong*, my current book, which is filled with symbols and deals with space and psychic phenomena."

Mary J. of Machipongo, Virginia, has many of the elements in the Star People profile, including a rare blood type and an extra vertebra. On May 1, 1978, Mary was involved in a serious automobile accident which placed her in the hospital for three months.

During the accident, Mary had an out-of-body experience:

"I saw myself above the car, watching my husband trying to control the vehicle after we hit an oil slick on a very rainy day. Then I floated through a black room and came upon a Light Being. The light from this entity was so bright that I remember putting my hands up to my eyes.

"Then I was out completely. I know God pushed me back for a reason. No one thought I would make it. Later, after two operations, no one could believe how quickly I healed. I'm a positive thinker with a lot of determination. I have had visions since I was about nine years old."

Lydia A.S. of Evanston, Illinois, remembers that before she was five years old, she felt as if she was never asleep.

"I had experiences of 'flying' at night over the small town in which we lived. I did not seem to be alone, but I don't have any memory of who it was who accompanied me.

"All of this stopped shortly after I was put into second grade at age five and a half. I could read at the age of three, and I was on third grade books before I started school. My teachers taught me to be 'reasonable.' "

German-born Gisela E. von S., now of California, is typical of the Star People who are convinced that either alone, or in the company of a guide, they are capable of visiting other worlds during out-of-body experiences.

"During some OBEs," Gisela feels, "I have visited Herkules, Uranus, Andromeda, and Antiobe. I have to admit that I knew about the existence of Uranus and Andromeda, but I had to find Herkules in my atlas-type star charts to be sure it was real. I could not find Antiobe at all, but I know that it exists. It is 'home.' "

"Many times OBE is accomplished when one is not consciously prepared", Francie has channelled. "Many people find themselves slipping out of the body during accidents or during acute suffering, illness, or exhaustion. Some feel great panic when they find themselves desperately attempting to 'paddle' their spiritual feet so that they might touch their room's physical floor. They are frightened when they discover they cannot control their spirit's comings and goings in the usual physical manner.

"In the spirit, one has but to *think* that he has moved to another area, and, instantly, the transportation is completed. In the spirit, one moves by thought, talks by thought-telepathy. Therefore it is important that, while in the spirit, one selects very carefully what it is that he most wishes to accomplish.

"Those who are unfamiliar with spirit-thought-travel may find themselves threshing about in windmill fashion to get to their still visible, very physical, front door. Then, to their amazement, they find themselves passing through the door without opening it—even though they might grimace, as if anticipating a collision. The physical dimension feels like a feather lightly touching when it passes over our spirit body.

"These inexperienced spirit travelers may try to shout messages to physical men and women they may see, who will be unable to hear a nonphysical voice. These naive spirit adventurers float, bounce, glide, and slide through trees and buildings, aimlessly wasting what could have been the most magnificent experience of their lives.

"When you spirit travel, remember to think of meeting with angelic beings, of going to the temple of love, wisdom and knowledge. These contacts will add to your life immeasurably, and you will more beautifully fulfill your Soul's mission to glorify the Source."

Chapter Twelve: Star People and Past Lives

As was revealed on the Starbirth questionnaire, Star People all accept the survival hypothesis of reincarnation of some aspect of rebirth of the Soul into a physical body.

Long before we had revealed the details of our Star People research, we had subjects breaking through the standard procedure of the regression experience to declare that they could now recall their true mission in life. Often this realization, this apparent memory activation of *why* they chose to come to Earth, would cause the subjects to weep. When the tears had subsided, though, the subjects would be filled with a comforting sense of well-being and resolution that their purpose in living would now be fulfilled. So many loose ends in their lives had been tied together by the knowledge that they were Starseed working their way back to their true homes.

This would seem to be the appropriate area to describe both our regression techniques and certain channelled materials pertinent to a clearer understanding of past lives.

*   *   *

Not long ago, a distraught mother came to us with her seventeen-year-old son, a depressed young man who had already made three suicide attempts. Five psychiatrists had each, in turn, given up on him. Depression perpetually clouded his life. The lad felt trapped in an inexorable pattern.

In one three-hour session, we enabled the teenager to view his "Karmic Counterpart," the former existence which was directly responsible for the imbalance in his present life experience. He left us, a smiling young man with a new perspective on life. A past-life recall permitted him to become integrated with his classmates and with society at large. The awareness this past-life gave him explained the many emotions—guilt, anger, passion, fear—that had always caused him great perplexity and turmoil. Thoughts of suicide and self-destruction have no place in his restructured personality.

A forty-year-old executive was pressured into seeing us by his wife, who had grown despondent with his apparent inability to display feelings of love. The man told us with a sneer of dismissal that "love was merely a head-trip."

After an altered-state induction had broken his psychic shell of emotional resistance, he expressed his catharsis in a release of tears. He emerged a man with vivid insight after recalling a past-life as a Franciscan monk, who had died defending a group of handicapped children who were being put to death by ignorant villagers.

He had been reluctant to show love in his present-life, but the process of regression had enabled him to see his actions as impediments to balancing the Karmic laws of compensation. He tearfully embraced his wife and expressed his desire to hurry back home to begin loving their children.

The young couple in their mid-twenties had reluctantly decided upon divorce as the only solution to their maladjusted marriage. Three psychologists and two marriage counselors had been unable to give them any practical assistance in healing the breach between them.

One session with each of them was all that was required to enable them to see that their lack of awareness of a previous, meaningful, shared, existence was now warping their opportunity to establish a fruitful relationship in their present-life experience. They resolved to recognize the lessons left unlearned from that other time, to benefit from the awareness gained, and they were certain that we had given them the proper tools to make their marriage truly work.

By utilizing altered-state-regression, we have worked with men and women from widely divergent backgrounds and enabled them to identify the solution to their present-life problems by gaining more complete knowledge of their past-life experiences. Participating in our regression sessions have been such diverse types of people as chemical company executives, attorneys, medical doctors, psychologists, nurses, school teachers, computer programmers, college professors, aerospace engineers, diamond merchants, garage mechanics, housewives, students, and servicemen and servicewomen.

Regardless of one's cultural, educational, or religious background, the symbol-system which we utilize is able to blend with the individual's world view and carry him or her to much wider and more universal places. We have embarked on what we call "The Starbirth Odyssey" with Baptists, Mormons, Lutherans, Roman Catholics, Methodists, Jews, and Sufis—and no one has found the odyssey incompatible with a personal cosmology. As Francie has said, "True awareness *enlightens* one's own path to the Source, so he may more clearly find it."

In our opinion, the true purpose of past-life exploration is to present the consultee with an awareness and with certain practical tools by which he might begin to solve his current life problems and enable him to build a more positive future.

The consultee is taken back to view, for his good and his gaining, aspects of the Karmic Counterpart, the past-life lived by his Soul that has sown the ignorance which he is reaping. Through a guided procedure which involves color, sound, music, and altered states of consciousness, the consultee achieves a balance with his present life.

The session is structured to encourage the consultee to remember his or her true purpose in life—why his Soul chose to put on the fleshly clothes of Earth and enter the reality of experience, the cause and effect found in the Karmic Wheel of material plane existence. This remembrance very often effectively answers the oft-heard plaint: "Why me?"

Throughout the regression the consultee receives valuable information about the ties which were experienced by his Soul's former relationship to family members and friends with whom he is *now* in contact. Such insights often permit the consultee to repair—or in certain cases to properly terminate—various relationships.

Every step of the process is taken with love and with words which encourage self-esteem, rather than ego. Along the way, the consultee is introduced to his "Guardian Angel," "Teacher," or "Guide," and, together, they choose former experiences to relive for the consultee's good and gaining. Exotic past-lifes, oriented for ego-manipulation, have never been explored during our regression sessions.

Whether reincarnation is fantasy or actual past lives led by the Soul coming forth as memory, many men and women have obtained definite and profound release of present-life pain and phobias by reliving the origin of the trauma in some alleged former existence. We have found that a prior belief in the theory of reincarnation is by no means necessary to permit the subject to experience a benefit from the cathartic vision.

Psychologists have long realized that discovering the *cause* of an existing condition very often releases the *effect* of its hold on a patient. Doctors know that diseases have emotional, as well as physical, origins and aspects.

By reliving an alleged past life, a subject is able to release fully his emotions and is able to accept responsibility for an action which he or she now considers already performed and done with in a previous lifetime. Once the consultee has made the transfer of responsibility for the trauma to the present life and has come to recognize that the "fault" and lack of awareness lies in a time far-removed from current concerns, he is able to deal with the matter without embarrassment or shame.

In a large sense, the Starbirth Odyssey offers the consultee an internal symbolical quest, permitting a deeper understanding of oneself, complete with a process of cleansing and purification.

Admittedly, it is an intensely spiritual voyage. But it is a journey which permits the consultee to return with a much clearer understanding of the language of his own mind and with a practical, working knowledge of his psyche's inner symbology. With such tools at one's disposal, the consultee is able to monitor personal progress on the path of effective growth throughout the rest of his or her life.

As I explained in *You Will Live Again*, when Francie revealed to me her vision that each person is but a "facet of his or her soul," her comments triggered a theory of mine regarding reincarnation which had occurred to me only after more than a decade of seriously researching the subject: Rather than each soul-personality reincarnating again and again to learn and to progress on the Earth plane, perhaps there may be a Soul-in-common shared by several materially manifesting personalities existing at different time sequences.

In other words, let us say that I seem to recall a life as a galley slave, circa 100 B.C.; a lifetime as a Viking, circa

1100 A.D.; an existence as a French diplomat, circa 1700; and a rugged time as a fur trapper, circa 1820. It may be that I, Brad Steiger, did not literally live those former lifetimes as the same personality being reborn, but that my present self-manifestation is able to tap into memories of growth and spiritual evolution which have been absorbed by a common Soul.

In this theory, the Soul may have materially expressed itself in hundreds of lifetimes and will have assimilated the growth memories acquired by each of those physical manifestations, but each of those personalities has lived but once.

It may be that the particular spiritual lessons learned by the galley slave, the Viking, the diplomat, and the trader are especially applicable to my present state of awareness, my present existence, but I was not actually any of those individuals in a previous life experience. I am only able to connect with certain "storage cells" of spiritual wisdom which are contained in the common Soul. Whether I spontaneously "tune into" these cells or whether I contact them through altered states of consciousness, the connection will aid in acquiring even more growth activity in my present Earth plane struggle.

Francie has stressed repeatedly that meditation is truly a necessity for awareness. Meditation is the quiet waiting to receive, for it permits contact with the Higher Self, where awareness can be gained from former lives led. Francie's vision of the true nature of the Higher Self, the Soul, has been expressed in *Reflections from an Angel's Eye*, a published collection of some of the teachings given her.

Here is the vision she was shown of the Higher Self and its incarnations. Forrest L. Erickson performed a PSE analysis of the following and found Francie free of deception.

"I was taken from my physical body to a realm far out in space, where I stood suspended. A living panorama was brought before me, a moving diagram, which provided me with many levels of awareness. I was shown an area in the upper righthand region, and I was told that it was a realm beyond ours, a space occupied by the Source, God.

"A golden cord extended down from that realm to the Higher Self, the Soul, which was represented by a large, glowing sphere. The golden cord was the umbilical cord that connects our Higher Self with God. The golden cord is our lifeline to the Source.

"Extending from the Higher Self were many silver cords, which formed starlike rays in every direction. They, too, were "umbilical cords" that connected each lifeform which had been entered into by the Soul. At the end of each silver cord, there existed smaller, crystal-like spheres, approximately twelve in number, which I was told represented each lifetime led on Earth.

"As I watched, an embryo formed within each of the spheres. The embryo became a child and matured to various ages. While each lifeform matured, it gathered knowledge, which was represented by sparkling lights around the sphere. Corresponding lights also became incorporated into the body known as the Soul, which was located at the hub of the model I was shown. As the lifeform grew in awareness, so, equally, did the Higher Self, the Soul. And as the lights came to be within the Soul, it grew to a more brilliant, vibrating intensity of white light. I knew its vibrations had increased from the knowledge gained by the lifeform.

"Upon the physical death of the lifeforms, I saw that some automatically became incorporated into the Soul, for they had been vibrating at a similar rate of awareness. Other lifeforms simply grew dark.

"This process continued throughout time, until all motion ceased to be. By then, the Soul had grown brilliant and was pulsating rapidly with the highest energies. It was magnificent to behold, as if it were a god.

"I was told that all Souls continue in this fashion, gathering vibrations until they raise their own energies with the many awarenesses gained by the various life-forms. The Souls thereby return to the Highest Vibration, the Source, more enriched than when they were created and sent forth.

"The judgment of each lifeform, concerning whether it will be incorporated into the Soul to be as gods, is one of self-judgment. Whether we vibrate with the higher awareness which may be gained from the wisdom of experience, or whether we remain ignorant, is of our own choice.

"Those lifeforms which had raised their vibrations, their awareness, were automatically incorporated into their Soul upon physical death. They will be permitted to join the Soul in its ascent to the Source.

"Those lifeforms which had chosen ignorance, remained dark, barely pulsating with energy. They were unable to become incorporated into the Soul. There must be another plan devised by the Source, other than Karma as we now know it, which will permit those who are now separate to one day become at one with All That Is.

"The relationship between our Higher Self and our spirit within us is one of a symbiotic nature. The Soul needs us as much as we need it. Through awareness gained from experience, we can raise our vibrations, become as one with our Soul, and ascend with it to the Source of all energy.

"The three wisemen of Christian tradition were led by a star to the Master Jesus so that they might give their gifts of gold, frankincense, and myrrh to the Source.

"The people of Earth will be led by the *Star* People to many levels of awareness so that they may bear the gifts of Love, Wisdom, and Knowledge to the Source."

Chapter Thirteen: Dreams of Remarkable Encounters

It came as no surprise to us to learn that the Star People dream often of UFOs and of encounters with alien beings.

The following account of such a dream was sent to us by Cindy J., a college student from Orange Park, Florida. Cindy's dream contains many elements which show up repeatedly in the reports which were supplied to us by the Star People.

"The setting was an amusement park. My mom, step-dad, seven-year-old brother, and I were having a good time. We were waiting in line to go on a ride when I heard someone yell, 'Look! Up in the Sky!'

"Coming through the clouds was a flying saucer. It hovered over the crowd, then it landed behind an old two-story building near the park. Everyone was very calm, more curious than anything else.

"The people started to move closer to the building. Many of these people had small children, under ten years of age, with them. I had become separated from my family, so I began moving toward the building.

"All of a sudden, people started screaming and yelling. Some force was pulling them toward the building and the UFO. Then I felt as though a million tiny hands were pushing and pulling me toward the house. There was a buzzing noise in my head and then the force was strong enough to pick me up off the ground. I tumbled and flew toward the doors of the building.

"The next instant I was inside the building and looking at the UFO. It was about twelve feet high and about twenty feet in circumference. It gave off a faint humming sound. There were a number of beings about four feet tall, dressed in layered clothing with hoods over their heads. Telepathically, I could understand them. They were taking care of the children they had drawn to them from the amusement park. Some of the beings were feeding the kids. Some were even changing diapers. One of them told me to help and to keep out of their way.

"There were babies and little kids all over, mostly lying down and sleeping. I walked up a staircase and found my baby brother upstairs. He was awake enough to ask me to tuck him in. He was right by a window. I looked out, and it seemed as though we were now in something that was moving very fast. There was a brilliant light all around us. I shrugged my shoulders and started tucking other kids in. No one was frightened."

Interestingly, a number of dreams the Star People have shared with us have portrayed them as being in amusement parks or in crowded streets. Both dream locales could represent the diverse, often chaotic, aspects of the world at large. When the UFO appears overhead, the basically calm response of the Star People is also typical, as is the UFO beginning to draw people toward, or up into, its interior.

The Star People seem always to be set to work by the

UFO entities which they encounter in their dreams. Cindy, like so many others, was told to make herself useful, and she did so by seeing that the younger children on board the craft were pacified.

Cindy's dream is also typical in that the UFO seems to serve as a symbol of deliverance from the chaotic "amusement park" world. The UFO is often a vehicle of transport, taking the dreamer and others to some unspecified, but nonthreatening, place.

Debra W. of Medford, Oregon, told us that, when she read of our work with the Star People, she put her head in her hands and cried out to her husband: "My God, you'll never believe what I am reading!"

For years, Debra told us, her husband Bob has informed her that he and his father were both of alien descent. Bob has nearly all of the identifying characteristics of the Star People and is "in tune with his distant brothers."

Debra made no claim of being a Star Person herself, but stated that "for some reason I seem to attract them."

She went on to inform us that she often dreams of UFOs and extraterrestrials. "I always see UFOs on the horizon, but in my latest dream, they landed on the street in front of our house. They came into the house, escorted us out, and took us all on a long journey with them. I don't remember where they took us, but I felt completely at peace.

"Since that dream," Debra revealed, "I have been much more aware of what goes on around me in the world today, and I know the UFOs are really coming soon, maybe within another five or six years. I would like to see them land tomorrow!"

A number of Star People have reported their dreams of witnessing great catastrophes and Earth Changes. In nearly all cases, they are busy helping others through the times of cleansing and purification.

A most intriguing aspect of the Star People's dreams has come to our attention since our photographs have appeared in print together with accounts of our research.

"The one dream I've had more than any other," wrote Carl A. to Francie, "is one of a great catastrophe. There is a woman there trying to get everyone to safety. She has the knowledge to save us all. I have had this dream many times, and now I know that the woman in my dreams is *you*. I recognize you from your picture in the newspaper."

"Several months ago," reported Carol D. of Warrington, Pennsylvania, "I bought Brad's book, *Alien Meetings*. It was put on the shelf with all my other books.

"In the early morning of September 29, I had a dream in which someone was trying to control my mind. The dream ended with my attending a meeting together with my father. There were about twenty people gathered, and you [Brad] were speaking to us. You were saying that there were those among us who were being tested. We were not to be frightened, as the test was only to teach us to control our thoughts. You handed me a book and told me to give it to my father. It was *Alien Meetings*.

"My parents visited me the next day. I was going to suggest that my father read your book, but I never got around to it. Later that evening, he came out of the den with *Alien Meetings* in his hand, sat down, and began to read. I told him about the dream, and he was stunned. I must have over 1500 books in my den, and he chose that particular one!

"The chapter which he was reading contained the accounts of the 'dreams' people were having in which they were aboard a UFO and were greeted by a man in a silver suit who they claimed was you. The detailed account and description given of the UFOs' interior is

almost exactly like the one I have entered in several
dreams that I have had over the last two to three years.''

Francie and I have both been rather astonished by the
number of letters which we have received from sincere
men and women, who, upon seeing our published
photographs, write to tell us that we are the ones who
have been instructing them in their dreams. In some
instances, they swear that they have had physical
encounters with us in which we have verbally relayed
important information of a highly spiritual nature.

Not long ago, I was making a number of media
appearances in a large southern city. I had enjoyed a bit
of repartee with the hostess of the local morning
television talk show, then I quickly left the studio for
the home of friends with whom I was staying.

No one at the studio knew where I was encamped, nor
had I released that information to anyone else in the
city. To further secure my privacy, my friends had an
unlisted telephone number.

I was in the process of changing clothes in the
guestroom when my host told me to pick up the
telephone extension. The phone was for me. A local
call.

I was, of course, puzzled. No one knew where I was
staying.

A woman's voice came over the receiver: ''Brad, I
was startled to see you on television this morning. You
are the man who appears in my dreams and teaches me.
The mustache [which I wore then], the gestures, the
facial expressions. It is you! But I did not know who
you were until I saw you on television this morning.''

I was so baffled that I could think of little to say. My
unknown ''student'' had no such impediment, for she
went on to relay a message that a ''Light Being'' had
told her to deliver to me. My solar plexus tingled when I
heard information that would fit precisely into a dif-

ficult problem with which I had been wrestling.

At last it occurred to me to ask a practical question of the young woman: "How did you know where to call me? How did you get this number?"

Her answer was that the same Light Being who had the message for me had also given her the number at which to telephone me.

The possibility that we might be appearing to men and women in the dream state is one thing, but it becomes a matter really quite difficult to manage when certain people insist that we have delivered teachings to them when we were in a physical state.

"The consultation you gave me was what saved my life," a woman told Francie a few months ago. "I know that I would have committed suicide had you not talked to me that night."

Francie searched the woman's face, smiled gently. "I'm sorry. You must be mistaken. Whoever your angel of mercy might have been, it wasn't I. We have never met before."

The woman crinkled her forehead in a ripple of hurt feelings and surprise. "It was in Santa Fe, Francie. You can't have forgotten me."

"I would never forget you," Francie consoled, placing a comforting hand on the woman's arm. "Brad," she smiled whimsically. "It's happened again."

It is truly difficult to explain the phenomenon to puzzled men and women when I do not really understand what is going on myself.

"But we met before in Santa Monica," someone will insist to me. "I was really low that day, down in the dumps. You came to me, introduced yourself, and said, 'Let's go have a cup of coffee and talk about your problem.' Lord, man, you really talked it all out of me and really helped me. And now, Brad, you say you don't remember me at all? Hey, man, I can't believe you could have taken our meeting so casually when it meant so much to me.''

People have sworn that they heard Francie and me lecture in small towns and cities in which we have never appeared. They praise us for the discussions we have led in study groups in cities and towns far from our usual circuit. They've been delighted with the time we have taken to answer questions until the wee hours of the morning.

Are we dealing with faulty memories, Brad-and-Francie imposters, or something that suggests the plastic nature of reality? We often dream of lecturing to both large and small groups of people. These dreams seem very real to us, and we often discuss them upon awakening.

Francie has received channelling to the effect that certain Higher Intelligences are using our images to provoke particular memories and responses in the Star People.

''It would be nice to say that our astral bodies, or whatever, are actually transporting themselves to all these people and teaching them,'' Francie has told me. ''I'm disappointed with what Kihief told me. I had hoped he would have said that, somehow, it was always us traveling to all those people. That way, Brad, we could be performing our mission of activating the Star People twenty-four hours a day!''

Rather, as Kihief told Francie, there is something about the arrangement of our features that seems familiar to many people. There is something about us that makes men and women feel as though they have known us before—in other lifetimes, on other worlds.

Also, as we become more well-known as writers and teachers in the metaphysical and inspirational fields, the angelic intelligences are using our images to reassure those who are becoming activated as Star People. When a seeker dreams of entering a UFO, he is reassured when he identifies "Brad Steiger" among the crew. When a dreamer receives a troubled view of the future and sees the time of cataclysms, he is comforted when he sees "Francie" leading crowds to safety. Truly, she must know the way, for she channels from a higher intelligence.

"But these visions and dreams usually have nothing to do with us as individuals," Francie once emphasized. "Angelic beings are simply using us, Brad. They are using our images to hasten contact with others who are needed to help bring about the Divine Plan."

We are not, then, great Master Teachers who have the ability to walk through Time and Space to aid others in their development. Our *images* are being utilized as activating mechanisms for the Star People.

"But what did Kihief say about the instances where people swear that they have encountered us in the physical body?" I pursued. "Isn't there, perhaps, bilocation going on in those cases?"

"It certainly would be nice to believe so," Francie admitted. "But, here again, it seems that the programming of the Star People is being accelerated at such a pace that, in many instances, dreams are becoming a significant part of the Greater Reality. Of course, in one sense, they always have been. Dreams have always been marvelous teaching mechanisms.

"What Kihief has told me," she further explained, "is that these lectures that we have given, these personal consultations that we have conducted, rarely take place in the physical, consensual, reality. Certain Star People are being given such powerful programming in their dreams, that, when they see our pictures in the various publications, their memories respond so dramatically that they are convinced that the dream-teachings were actual physical happenings. They are certain that they have actually met us and received personal contact from us."

* * *

Interestingly, I had no sooner written the above when a letter arrived from Kathy S. of Sioux Falls, South Dakota, which beautifully illustrated the dream-vision mechanism.

"My son and I had returned from dinner and were sitting in the living room discussing a concert," Kathy writes. "My mind was far from esoteric things. As I walked into the kitchen, I was confronted by a life-sized apparition of you [Brad Steiger] dressed as a monk. You were in an environment of small hills and olive trees, and you were aglow in a sort of filtered golden light.

"I was immersed in a tremendous wave of warmth and love as you stated (telepathically), 'I am Brother Thellonius.' (Or Thessalonius, I didn't quite get the name.)

"The image was not at all startling. It seemed very matter of course. Later that evening, during meditation, I was shown a lovely scene of otherwordly things and the same voice of you as the monk saying: 'You have seen the true reality. No matter what might befall your physical vision, you *will see* the true reality.'

"Later still, as I was on the verge of falling asleep, the monk appeared again, and I seemed to be levitated about three inches above the bed.

"Brad, as the monk, you appear *exactly* as you do in current photos—even your hair is the same. I don't know if this is significant to you, but I personally feel that there is a very high spirit entity communicating through you—seemingly a philosopher of ancient Persia or thereabouts, who makes himself known to those who can discern the 'true reality.' "

Francie on dreams:

During the dream state we are totally receptive to any thought that our mind might wish to receive. The dream and the trance-like states offer particularly good times for our angelic beings to interact with us. During those times in which our physical bodies lie dormant, involved in repetitious movement, or open to hypnotic induction, we can be set free of the normal limitations of reality. Thought-awareness will better be able to affect our lives on many levels.

During wakefulness, each of us has certain shells of varying thicknesses which we erect around ourselves. These shells are often necessary to protect us from the many assaults to be found in daily living. Regretfully, it is this same protective shell which so often blocks contact with the other side. Setting aside time for meditation will permit one to reach a state of consciousness to receive awareness, but the dream-state will still provide one of the most productive areas in which to receive teachings.

Visual teachings from beyond most often come in symbol-language. This language is best described as single images which represent whole thought forms. The ability to understand your individual symbol-language takes but a few minutes daily.

Keep a notepad on your bedside table, together with a small file box with cards tabbed from "A" to "Z." Each night before you retire, date the notepad.

When you awaken, record your dream. Underline the subject matter.

For instance, let us say that you were purchasing new shoes in your dream, because the shoes you were presently wearing were damaged. You tried on many pairs of shoes before choosing a pair that felt the most comfortable. Now underline the subject matter, *damaged shoes exchanged for new shoes*. Think of what "shoes" may represent.

Shoes are your foundation. They permit you to walk comfortably wherever you choose to go.

Remember, you tried on many shoes until you found a pair that was comfortable. Trying on several pairs may indicate that you will have to try many paths. You should change to a new way of going in which you will feel more comfortable, because the way you are now walking is damaging to your awareness (remember the *damaged* shoes in your dream).

On an index card, you should write: *"Shoes."* Beneath the topic, write, *"Damaged shoes exchanged for new shoes.* I should change my way of going for another, more comfortable, way."

Now file this card under "S" for shoes.

Each dream has major subject matter. Nearly all events symbolically received can be filed by the particular subject, its meaning, and how it directly relates to your personal experience.

I do not wish to influence your own personal dream symbology, but here are a few subjects most often dreamed of by sensitive men and women and the meanings which I have come to recognize in a large number of consultations:

Trees: People, living lifeforms, whose outstretched arms reach to the Source of energy. Low branches indicate people who are easy to reach, to whom you can easily relate. Trees with high branches represent those people who are difficult to reach.

Mountain: Master Teacher or wisdom from the Source.

Water: Creative energy. If the water is muddy or if it is clear will indicate to you how you are using your creative energy.

Food: That which we take into ourselves daily, such as attitudes of those around us.

Attacking Animals: Hostile people or problems.

Birds: Messages of awareness flying toward you from beyond.

Doors: New ways open to you.

The manner in which the subject matter normally relates to you is usually the measure of understanding its meaning.

If you should dream that you have mud all around

you, you would best understand this image by realizing how you would react—and what state of affairs you would be in—if mud really were all around you. You might feel that there was no path out of the dilemma. Therefore, in the waking state, you would have to seek a way out of circumstances which your dream showed as "mud" surrounding you.

If you should dream of being all alone in a boat in the middle of a large body of water, you may feel that in the waking state you are helpless to use properly the creative energy that is all around you. Give of your creative energies during the day, and you will find your life becoming more positive and productive.

After even a few nights of productive dreaming, you will find your file box beginning to fill up with your dream symbols and their subjective meaning to you. You will be able to flip to any subject matter and recall what it means in your life.

After a period of about a month, you will have memorized your symbolic dream language, and you will have become more aware of everything about you. You will know much more clearly what you must do. You will have received a glimpse of what is in store for you in your future. And it will have become easier for the angelic beings to speak to you, to teach you, to prepare you, and to guide you throughout your life.

In addition to the normally received symbol-system which so many other people have also acquired, the Star People are in attunement with other types of images. These images are inherited and are contained within the chromosomal, genetic structures, which have been passed on to us by our ancestors. These bits of encapsulated awareness trigger the Star People awake to their purpose, their obligation to their fellow Earthlings. These special symbols program the Star People to become actively involved in aiding others.

It is after receiving this inherited awareness that the Star People become the media through which the vibrations of Love, Wisdom, and Knowledge can flow, affecting all those with whom they come into contact. It is after this awakening that the Star People become Light Bearers to illuminate the Paths of Awareness to the Source for all to see more clearly.

As I have stated, the Star People's triggering symbol-system is one that is linked to dormant memories. There is no interpretation necessary, for what is imaged indicates what the Star Person is to remember through the linkup with the ancestral Sowers or Initiates.

Here are some of the images and remembered scenes which awaken the Star People and bring out the pro-grammed teachings and awareness:

A crystal city
A classroom
Sitting with a berobed or spacesuited teacher
Meeting a High Being aboard a UFO
A feeling of oneness with animals that permits communication with them
A sky bearing two moons
A new planet coming into vision
Crashing from the sky
A massive fire surrounding oneself in a space vehicle
An alien home planet beyond the stars
Meeting a more perfect image of oneself
Moving through the rainbow and feeling its varied vibrations go through you
Traveling to another planet or another dimension, recognizing many people, and finding that place to be your true home

Chapter Fourteen: Becoming a Star Person

Francie's Techniques for Preparing Spirit, Mind, and Body for Becoming a Star Person:

There are many entities of varying functions who have been interacting with humankind for aeons. Certain of these beings are concerned with our awareness, our spiritual advancement. These beings have the ability to defy solid matter, coming and going instantly, heeding not our physical laws as they enter our homes without means of a door.

With training and diligent practice you, too, can step from your earthly shells and travel with them. You can accompany them to the Golden Temple of Love, Wisdom, and Knowledge, and there receive the beautiful teachings given. However, you must then return and set about to aid others to become more aware. You must shine a light so that others might more clearly see their individual paths of awareness which lead to the Source.

Feel not alone or unusual when visiting with the Angelic Entities. Throughout its history many of the Earth's greatest personages have interacted with these angelic beings. The world's most reknowned leaders and spiritual teachers talked of meetings with the angels. Socrates, George Washington, Nikola Tesla, Da Vinci, Raphael, Emerson, Joan of Arc, Swedenborg, Bernadette of Lourdes, and countless others spoke of contact with these beautiful beings. Mankind's most famous leaders, inventors, musicians, writers, poets, scientists, and political leaders have been visited by angelic entities. Our most influential thinkers have been inspired to do their greatest works through these intelligences. The bibles of many cultures contain accounts of numerous interactions with these beings, and the teachings they shared are still taught today. For these entities wish to help all of humankind enrich our lives with their wisdom and to make us more aware, so that we may more greatly glorify the Source—God.

Such contact is possible for all who sincerely desire such communication. Within all of humankind there exists the ability to enter a dimension which operates on a higher vibration, where unconditional love, wisdom, and knowledge can be received.

Accomplishing the following steps will enable you to enter this domain, and once there, you will be able to control material reality and transcend to the space beyond the physical so that you can live a more meaningful and productive life.

First, you must know truly what it is that you are seeking. What it is that you may expect to see, hear, and know. This is the anatomy of a vision.

Most teachings are given in visual-thoughtform. Some are also accompanied by a verbal explanation.

You will be transported to a beautiful realm in space where a magnificent, colorful panorama of living diagrams and thought-teachings are given, or you will receive these teachings while seated comfortably in the Temple of Love, Wisdom, and Knowledge, where many join you to receive.

While in this timeless domain, a feeling of unconditional love will permeate your entire being. This is the dimension where the angelic beings interact with you, share with you, teach you all you will need to know. Yet, what is given here cannot be contained. It must not be permitted to stagnate. It must be shared with others. In the giving, you will receive anew. You must give to receive.

Feelings of love, oneness, ecstasy, and indescribable joy are all pervasive here. These feelings are so overwhelming that nothing else in the world seems important. They are so encompassing that there is left no emptiness, no hunger, no longing for anything else. For the first time in your life you feel complete, you feel whole. This feeling of love is experienced with such great intensity, such immeasurable happiness, that it will engulf you totally; there exists no greater feeling.

You are totally happy on the one hand for the contact having occurred, but there is also a deep sadness, a longing, for the precious time that elapsed before such contact was made. Both of these intense emotions are felt at once. One's mouth seems to open wide to wail, to mourn, to laugh, and to shout for joy for love of God. This feeling accompanies all contact with Higher Intelligence and all vision-teachings. One need never ask another whether or not a teaching received is truth, for with this feeling of love and joy, truth cannot be mistaken. Every cell in the physical body vibrates with this unconditional love.

This beautiful realm was created by the Angels so that there might be an idyllic, heavenly domain in which teachings might better be received. This place permits the seeker to have a more receptive mind. It is singularly awesome and magnificent in splendor.

The angelic entities often appear as familiar religious figures we esteem highly—such as a particular saint, guru, holy figure, master.

Christians, especially children, report seeing Jesus. Many Christians have reported that they felt the figure seen was Jesus, even though he did not really resemble the many drawings which represent him. Rather, more accurately, a feeling of "knowing" seemed to be implanted into their consciousness that they were beholding Jesus or one who vibrated with the unconditional love that Jesus emitted.

Logically, it is obvious why such a method might be employed by the angelic beings. Wouldn't we better accept guidance, words of wisdom, or love from someone whom we already loved, respected, and knew?

Yet, we must consider that these religious figures, these beloved holy ones whom we meet, might truly be those very esteemed individuals, with whom we can interact while penetrating their domain in a state of altered consciousness.

It is interesting to speculate on why the person, represented by the angelic beings, is one that is of the highest order in one's religious construct. Rarely, indeed, does the orthodox Jew see Jesus, the Buddhist see Mohammed, the Christian see Buddah, or the Hindu see Allah. All those of religious orientation report to have "seen" their holy representative when they were given teachings of Unconditional Love, Wisdom, and Knowledge.

The teaching that is given to you will come in a matter of minutes, two, three, or ten at the most, rarely more—though you may feel twenty minutes have expired or you may slip into a gentle sleep thereafter and be unable to determine time at all. This is a truth that is universal, for in that other domain, in the altered states of consciousness, there exists no feeling of time. Time, as we know it, is of the physical domain.

This is why there is frequently an error in judgment in the predicting of an event. Unless a specific date is given by the Beings, or unless the envisioned scene depicts the time, it is impossible to guess the exact time the event will occur. Sometimes you can accurately "guess" when the event might occur by the clothing of the people shown, by the buildings depicted, by what the people are doing, or by a "feeling" of the approximate time it might occur.

When receiving a teaching-vision, a feeling of "knowing" develops from two main factors. You will feel that you have *known* the teaching before, and you will have an inner belief that what you have seen is *truth*. You will feel it in your heart and in your stomach. Both will vibrate together, and no one will shake you from that belief.

There exists one more dimension that fully describes a vision-teaching.

When questioned by anyone about what you have received, heard, seen, you will be able to answer beyond that which you consciously realized. You will have the ability to answer questions which go beyond your vision; for in receiving a teaching-vision, you also absorb the frequencies that accompanied the teaching, thereby elevating your own vibrational awareness. You are, therefore, able to comprehend more than you could have understood at the moment the vision was received. You can then view the teaching from other perspectives, thereby achieving a greater depth of understanding.

In relating the vision-teaching, you become more aware of the entire truth envisioned. For in the giving, you receive afresh—and in greater abundance. Vision-teachings are living vibrational truths composed of varying levels, and depending on your awareness, you perceive the level of truth nearest your own understanding. Yet it is one.

All truth-teachings are separate to our understanding and perception, yet they are connected one to the other and thereby appear to grow in depth and complexities until one's awareness permits him to reach the One Truth in its totality—God.

When your vibrational awareness increases, you will become more in tune with your Higher Self. Remember, since your Higher Self contains the learning and awareness had from many lifetimes, you will be more able to attune yourself to these memories and awarenesses. Contact with the Higher Self's wisdom also permits you to become more aware and to more fully comprehend what you have seen in the vision-teaching. All these aspects merge together and will aid in leading you to the Source—God.

The receiving of a teaching-vision comes when you are practicing a form of meditation.

Prayer is not meditation. Simply said, Prayer is sending; Meditation is receiving.

Prayer is pleading, speaking. Meditation is receiving, listening.

Never enter meditation with a question, for this constitutes prayer and involves the ego. Never begin by telling the angelic beings what you wish to know about, what you wish to receive from them; for with hope, wonder, and desire, one's ego can be said to block, to interfere. It is then possible for our intricate brain to recreate the desired answers in our own prejudiced belief construct. For our minds use desires as their fuel. Excessive ego can terminate contact. Retain humility.

If any thought enters your mind, you should gently remove it. Do this very gently, though, for you should never attempt to shove an intruding thought away. Instead, tell the thought that you will think of it later, then gently push it from your mind.

Cleanliness within and without is important. Begin by readying your temple, your body. First clean your body physically. The desire to cleanse yourself within will follow. One cannot stand filth or stagnation within when truly cleansed without.

I have been told that a vegetarian diet will best prepare you for creating a temple that will house the higher vibrations. It will ready your body, which will reflect into the mind and into your spiritual awareness. One should not partake in the death, the suffering, or the destruction of a fellow creature with which one shares the Earth. We must know and practice all-consuming Unconditional Love for *all* living things, and we cannot do this while devouring them.

One should develop the ability to deny all past conditioning that has been drummed into his head. One should have the determination to clear his thoughts. An open mind is essential and ideal when one seeks contact with the angelic beings. One must be prepared to become far more aware than he previously dreamt was possible.

Open yourself truly to receive all there is.

Begin with a prayer of love, asking for guidance. Request protection from the chaotic vibration which humankind has caused to exist as a result of its ignorance. Pray fervently for a few minutes, then bathe in the enveloping, warm, soft love and protection which prayer permits.

Many props may aid you in achieving the required state of relaxation. Background music; flickering, revolving lights; luminous stars that glow from your ceiling; candles; etc. These stimuli will intensify your belief construct and aid you in projecting yourself to the other domain. All these materials will help to put your physical desires and physical body to sleep while awakening your spiritual self, your true self.

Each time the steps are followed, the more effective they will become. As you come truly to believe in these techniques, the concentration time will become shorter and the realization will become heavier. Soon you will be able to thought-travel, for you are preparing yourself and training your mind. You will reach the other dimension where the angelic beings await you. With fervent practice of the Three Steps to Awareness, you will become a purer person, a clearer channel. You will become more highly attuned—both mentally and spiritually—to receive the higher vibrations.

For those of you who find it difficult to "see," know that you will be able to visualize. We have worked with people who stubbornly spoke of seeing nothing but darkness when they closed their eyes. Yet, through diligent practice in creating images and in visualizing, they can now see.

Most people can see vague outlines of images against a dark background. This is the first step toward perceiving true visions. The second step will permit the viewer to see the images more clearly. A definite distinction becomes evident, as the images become bolder against a vaguer background. A third step allows colors to filter through, pale at first, later intensifying and becoming prismatic in their array. The last step is to become part of the image. The Three Steps will aid you in achieving visualization, as it is a process which permits you to transcend the physical reality for the true reality. It is a psychic pump that permits visual images to flow. Soon you will step beyond the image conjured and walk into the other world to view that which you could never dream.

Whether you are taken to the Golden Temple to receive your vision-teachings, whether you are taught by a bubbling brook, or whether you are permitted to stand in space among the stars will not matter, for all truths can be received in any of these places.

It is uncanny just how many people who, spontaneously and independently of one another, have been taken to the Golden Temple. They have all described the sparkling texture of the winding halls that lead to a central chamber and the many berobed figures gathered there to receive.

Before we began to take others to the realm beyond to meet their teachers and other angelic beings, we were unaware that anyone other than ourselves had seen this Temple of Love and Truth. In fact, when I first met Brad, I was astonished to hear him refer to the same Golden Temple of Love, Wisdom, and Knowledge. He had envisioned the Temple in the beautiful teaching dreams he had since childhood.

We both described the temple as being golden in color, but I had noted that, upon closer scrutiny, the substance of the building seemed to be of a semi-translucent material, such as opaque crystal or white marble. The golden hue turned out to be a reflective one, in that the temple was bathed in a golden, aura-like light. Each of us had seen a winding hallway leading to a large central chamber where many figures in robes gathered.

In certain instances, a Master Teacher instructs the students gathered around him. At other times, we agreed, a bright ray of light comes in the midst of the students gathered, and teachings issue from that source. The Temple is located in a magnificent lush garden. To the left of the main entrance, a lovely brook runs through the grounds. I was once told that all this exists in a region called "Lealand," in a place "like-unto-Venus."

When, in altered states of consciousness, we took others to meet the angelic beings, we were in awe to hear them describe the same scenes, word for word: the garden, the brook to the left of the Temple, the composition of the temple, how it was structured within and without, the many robed figures gathered there. We now believe, more firmly than before, that, in some other realm, this very place truly exists.

Visiting this Temple permits you to elevate continuously your vibrations, strengthen the connection that exists between your Higher, more Perfect Self—your Soul—and to achieve your birth in the stars.

It becomes extremely important to practice the Three Steps to Awareness at this particular time, for during the 1980s and 1990s there must be many helpers. Earth will be reaping the vibrations it has sown, for being physical, it, too, is tied within the Karmic laws of cause and effect. Continuously practicing the elevation of your awareness will permit you to become a Star Person, one of the survivors who will herald in the New Age.

The Three Steps to Awareness permits you to achieve an even greater awareness, thereby raising your vibrations beyond this lesser place, this confined reality. You will be able to understand the true reasons for certain events in your life. You will become more capable of changing those things that have caused you to stagnate and to stand still on the path that leads to the

Source. You will gain a feeling of mission, of purpose, of self-worth. You will lose the pretense of ego that blocks and consumes you. You will achieve a greater perspective and come to know of unconditional love, wisdom, and knowledge. You will evolve as a more perfect instrument for the Source to utilize for the glory of all creation.

Before you relax into a comfortable position for meditation, it is often good to loosen all major body parts and all appendages. By doing so, you will be releasing any restrictions which may have manifested in stiffness and blockage in your body. You will also be permitting fresh oxygen to nourish you. Breathe deeply and slowly as you rotate your body parts.

Visualize your body describing a circle as you bend from the hips and swing your torso in a clockwise movement. Breathe in as you begin the circle, breathe out as you complete the other half. Do everything slowly.

While performing the circles, close your eyes. You are creating a circle, an entire, whole movement. Think of the Whole, the complete Oneness of God. With each completed circle, think of the Whole energy of God coming into your being.

Without consciously counting, complete approximately nine circles, first in one direction, then the other. Create a circle to the best of your ability. Your circles will increase in perfection as you practice this movement.

Then, to a count of nine, rotate every movable part of your body, first in one direction, then the other. Create a circle with each of your fingers, your wrists, ankles, knees, elbows, shoulders, hips, neck, waist, even your toes. Keep the movements slow, comfortable, circling freely, easily, glorifying the Source.

Chapter Fifteen: The Three Steps to Awareness

The following is a method of achieving awareness which was given to Francie. It has aided all those who have sincerely practiced it. It is also one of the cassette tapes within the *Starbirth Odyssey* album which we have created to help activate the Star People. You may also create your personalized tape by reading slowly the following method against some soft background music, while recording it on your own machine. Then listen and follow it, and you will take a major step toward achieving a higher reality.

Choose a quiet place for your spiritual trek.

Lie down or recline comfortably and permit your body to begin to relax. If you have a cassette tape or a record of long-playing, tranquil, meditative music, affording you at least thirty minutes of sound, consider allowing music to assist you in relaxing and transcending the physical.

This is the technique that affords you the ability to transcend beyond:

Close your eyes and picture yourself breathing in pure, cleansing air. Visualize it entering your *left* nostril. Imagine the air filtering through your brain, through all of your thoughts, throughout your entire body, picking up any and all darkness and negativity, all body impurities. Visualize that darkened air leaving through your *right* nostril. In through the left—cleansing, purifying air—and out through the right.

Imagine the air that comes out your right nostril being dark at first, then becoming gradually lighter as it cleanses your entire being, both mentally and physically. With continual slow, rhythmic breathing, the air will become gradually clean.

Breathe in clean air and breathe out clean air, until a cycle, round-and-round, in-and-out, is formed. Continue this until approximately ten minutes of breathing has taken place.

Now, imagine yourself venturing forth on your Spiritual Odyssey, berobed in pure, shining, protective white.

Begin walking slowly, purposefully, through an enchanted forest. You are following a golden light, and you are treading a path lined with beautiful trees of all types, sizes, and varieties.

See the branches of the trees. They are very low, low enough to reach and to touch. You are able to touch them without straying from the straight path, two feet wide, that leads you through the forest.

Look at the bark of the tree. Although some of the trees have a rough, exterior bark, you are able to see the soft, inner core beneath, which gives off a glow where the life force exists.

Continue walking and look to your left.

Beside the path sits a small bear cub. It is friendly and playful. Reach down and pat it, and watch it respond lovingly.

Walk on, following the golden light.

Ahead is a beautiful lake, filled with sparkling, clean water, which comes from a mountain stream. The lake nurtures multicolored, lively fish, and it empties out into the Ocean of Life.

As you stand before the pulsating Ocean of Life, reach into your robe, just over your heart, and remove a drinking cup that rests there. Your cup.

Hold it heavenward and psychically, mentally, shout up the words: "Love! Love! Love!"

As you watch the sky above you, you see a beautiful love vibration gathering from the four corners of the heavens. One bright ray of light comes from the North, another from the South, another from the East, and again, another from the West.

They meet, merge, and form one almost blinding ray of white light.

This ray is filled with heavenly love, from the angelic beings, and it is beaming down to you.

It is splashing into your cup, filling it as it transforms itself from light to a milky-pink nectar.

It flows into your cup until it runs over the brim and annoints you.

Now lower the cup to your lips and drink the nectar. Drink it all. Drink down this delicious heavenly love, which bears an apricot-like taste. Feel how it glows and warms every part of your body.

Look at your cup. See how it has changed.

Look within it and without. See how it has been transformed from holding this pure and heavenly love.

Put your cup back inside your robe and enjoy the warmth.

This is the first step to awareness.

Next, feel yourself begin to float. You are rising higher and higher.

As you look up, you see a huge, glowing cloud descending to meet you. It is white, tinged with gold.

You rise higher. It comes nearer. When you reach it, you climb aboard and rise even higher.

You are rising above Earth. You are rising above the clouds. You are rising higher and higher, higher and higher.

You move beyond the Earth, beyond the stars, beyond this dimension. Moving through many Levels of various colors to reach the beautiful Crystal City in the sky.

Step off the cloud and see before you a Crystal River of cleansing, sacred holy water.

This holy, healing water cleanses within as well as without. It removes all scars, hurts, pains, regrets, burdens, and leaves you clean.

Wash yourself. Dip your whole body into the water. It is the perfect temperature, and it only rises as high as your heart.

If you have any troublesome or annoying habits, addictions, or appearance problems wash them away, too, and watch them float away downstream.

Then, clean and pure as a newborn baby, get out of the holy, healing water, the inner baptism, and walk to the opposite shore.

This is the second step.

It is at this time that you can make decisions without regret. If you have a problem you wish to solve, a decision you need to make, leave it floating on the water.

As you stand on the opposite shore, see it bobbing on the holy water, awaiting your decision.

You are now facing the problem, but you are detached, separate from it. You have severed its emotional attachment to you.

Know that God is goodness!

Face the problem floating on the water, and say this: "In the name of God, if it is for my good and my gaining, rise!

"In the name of God, if it is *not* for my good and my gaining, sink and be gone from me!"

If the problem rises, return to the water, snatch it from the air, and clutch it to your bosom. It is for your good and your gaining.

You may test the problem again in the same manner whenever doubt arises concerning whether or not you should continue to carry the problem with you.

If the problem sinks and is gone from you, let it go. Do not return to the water. The problem may be for another to bear, but it is not for you.

Once you have made your decision—or if there is no problem to test—turn away from the holy, healing water and climb the opposite bank. Walk up a grassy knoll.

As you climb toward its top, program yourself positively. Be truly proud of your efforts toward self-improvement. Vow to move away from any negative, unwanted habits.

Now, at the top of the hill, you see a beautiful, golden chalice, bedecked with jewels. The huge chalice is filled to the top with a golden substance. It is a distillation of the highest love available—Unconditional Love. This love will transform you, for it is even above that of heavenly Love. It is directly from the *Source*.

You have been filled with heavenly, angelic love.

You have cleansed yourself in the Crystal River, washing yourself within as well as without. You have made any necessary decisions without regret with Divine Help.

Now drink from the Golden Chalice of God's Love. Drink every drop of it.

Vow from this moment on to be as a kettle or teapot of unconditional love.

Whenever you interact with any living thing, picture yourself as a tea kettle of love, complete with a spout. Periodically image yourself pouring out unconditional love on that person, animal, or plant.

Unconditional, heavenly love flows in through the top of your head, filling you totally, to the very brim. You pour out love to all of life through the spout, where your heart is.

Every drop that is given from the spout is immediately replenished through the top.

Remember that just as it is impossible to fill a teapot to its brim by pouring in the spout, so is it impossible to be filled with earthly love through the heart. The deep, inner hunger can only be filled by God's love, which comes in through the top.

Become an instrument of God's love, perfect love. If someone rejects your love, your sharing, be not hurt or rejected. You will be instantly filled through the top with God's love.

Never give love expecting a return from earthly love. The love of a mate, a child, a parent, a friend is a bonus while on the Earth-plane. But that deep longing can only be satisfied by God's love. One should never expect to fill his kettle from the spout.

When you reach a greater understanding, you will be able to image your spiritual tea kettle on even inanimate things. All will be in balance, for you will be vibrating with the highest attunement in the universe—love!

This is the third step.

Now, set the chalice down and look toward the horizon. See looming up from the midst of the Crystal City the great spires of the magnificent Golden Temple. Rush to the temple. You are now prepared to enter into its vibration.

See before you a gigantic golden door, nine feet high, three feet wide. It is open.

Enter and discover the three highest vibrations— Love, Wisdom, Knowledge.

Awaiting you within is your Higher Self, your Guardian Angel, your Master Teacher.

You will learn your true purpose on Earth. You will remember your mission.

You will discover how you must accomplish what you need to do. If there are any past-life experiences directly related to your present-life experiences, you will learn of them here.

All you learn here will be for your good and your gaining. And all these things will prepare you for your birth in the stars—your Starbirth!

Chapter Sixteen: Special Gifts

Although her principal mission is to serve as a channel for angelic intelligence, Francie also has the special gift of prophecy. For more than twenty years, her prophetic talents had been shared privately with friends, family, and those who sought her out for consultations. But, in the spring of 1978, Kihief told her that she might answer the requests of various national tabloid newspapers and radio programs, which had been asking her to make public predictions. Kihief said that she could become a public prognosticator for a period of about a year, *solely* for the purpose of calling attention to her more serious work of channelling angelic teachings.

From her earliest memory, Francie has disclosed, she desired to affect the greatest change for the multitudes that she could possibly accomplish. She wanted somehow to bring about some wonderful discovery or deed.

"By the age of nine," she remembered, "I was enamored of medicine. I read every medical book that I could understand. I believed that one day I might invent a vaccine for one of the many dreaded diseases that plague mankind.

"Recently," she reflected, "when I channelled for various public media and released the prediction concerning the hyperthermic treatment of cancer patients, I had to smile at my innocent ignorance. I had felt with all my being at that tender age that I would wage a fight against physical disease. Now I realize that I am waging a war against even deadlier adversaries—ignorance, lack of awareness, prejudice, and negativity. These elements also constitute terrible plagues on Earth, and through my continuing interaction with angelic beings, I am channelling the 'vaccine' of enlightenment."

A prediction that Francie repeated many times in the fall of 1978 was that the winter of 1978–1979 would be exceedingly severe. She also stated that the entire year of 1979 would be marked by freak weather conditions. Both in print and on the air, she warned again and again that people should prepare for a long, harsh winter.

On January 1, 1979, Northern Europe was paralyzed by freezing storms. Hundreds of rail, bus, and automobile passengers in England and Denmark were stranded in snowbanks. Twenty-five seamen from the Greek supertanker *Andros Patria*, together with the wife and child of the ship's captain, were listed as missing off the coast of northwest Spain. Southern Sweden was paralyzed by the storm, and helicopters had to rescue eighty Soviet seamen from two trawlers that ran aground.

By January 7, the storm had become Europe's worst in fifteen years and had invaded the balmy climate of the Mediterranean. Authorities stated that 141 people died in the ice, snow, and cold and that they dug out 4,000 vehicles and helped over 8,000 persons.

Given that fierce advent, the winter continued with heavy blizzards and freezing temperatures across the nation and throughout Europe.

In 1979, April showers did not bring May flowers.

On May 2, two inches of snow fell in England and Wales.

On May 12, record cold temperatures moved across Louisiana, Georgia, North Carolina, and Florida. Golf-ball-sized hail pelted Central Florida, and a sultry heat spell in Louisiana was instantly snapped to record lows.

On June 26, Baltimore set a record low of 54 degrees. In the Adirondacks, the temperature plummeted to 28. Albany plunged to a record low of 41. In Concord, New Hampshire, the mercury dipped to just below 32 degrees, their coldest June 26 on record.

In mid-July, Cheyenne, Wyoming, endured the first tornado in its history. Hailstones as large as grapefruit bombarded the community of Fort Collins, Colorado, and turned the hospital emergency room into what looked like a battle zone.

On August 12, normally "dog days" for the Midwest, the temperatures fell into the 30s from North Dakota to upper Michigan and south to Kansas. A light frost covered most of northern Minnesota, and it fell to 28 degrees at the community of Embarrass. Dodge City, Kansas, had to weather a record low of 50 degrees.

In late 1978, Francie predicted in various media that the Third World would begin to suffer a famine that would eventually affect and afflict the entire globe.

On November 11, 1979, Eduard Saouma, Director-General of the United Nations Food and Agriculture Organization in Rome, announced that approximately 400 million people suffered from serious malnutrition. The Director-General stated that this massive food shortage will increase the role of America as the world's breadbasket, but might possibly result in economic disaster in the next twenty years.

Francie predicted in print that many rivers in the United States would be found to be carrying radioactive wastes.

Late in 1979, rivers in California, Arizona, and New Mexico were found to be contaminated by the irresponsible release of radioactive wastes. A radioactive chemical with a half-life of 16.4 million years was discovered to have contaminated three square miles of the Snake River Aquafier below the Idaho National Engineering Laboratory. Iodine 129 was measured in a concentration more than twenty-five times the allowable standards for drinking water.

Francie foresaw that industry would respond to the fuel crisis by creating energy sources from garbage. She repeated this prognostication several times early in 1979.

On November 11, the *New York Times* carried a story about Michael Dingman and his Refuse Energy Systems Company in Saugus, north of Boston. According to the account, Dingman provides fuel for thirteen North Shore communities and to General Electric's jet engine plant. "Rubbish is more reliable than oil," the *Times* quotes Dingman. "Why bury it?"

Also on the energy scene, Francie envisioned the commercial sale of "gasohol."

By the end of 1979, gasohol was being sold at hundreds of stations in the Midwest and was in the embryo stages in such states as Arizona. Chrysler and General Motors broadened their warranties to permit gasohol in their cars and trucks.

Concerned about the dietary intakes of men and women in contemporary society, Francie warned that dangerous toxins would be found in our meats.

In January 1979, a government study indicated that fourteen percent of all dressed meat and poultry being sold in supermarkets may contain illegal residues of chemicals suspected of causing cancer, birth defects, and other toxic effects.

In order to escape the rising costs of living, Francie saw many households exploring the possibilities of underground homes. Industry, she noted, would experiment with a shorter work week.

On July 29, 1979, United Press International carried a feature on the underground construction of homes. Interviews with prominent architects revealed that they receive ten to thirty calls and letters per day requesting building plans for underground homes. The architects stated that they knew of subsurface construction going on in Wyoming, North Dakota, New York, Pennsylvania, California, Connecticut, Massachusetts, and Oregon.

By late 1979, shorter work week experiments had been reported in several states by major companies and industries.

Early in 1978, Francie predicted in print and on the air that a combination of heat, microwaves, and high frequency sound would destroy cancer cells.

The winter issue, 1979, of *Science Digest* told of the partial realization of that prediction. According to that magazine, hyperthermia, or heat therapy, is being used to destroy cancer cells while leaving healthy tissues intact. Other therapists were also reported utilizing high-frequency sound waves and microwaves to destroy malignancies.

A prognostication that Francie repeated frequently cautioned against excessive protein intake and went on to state that our own body protein would be found to be a culprit in many diseases.

The October 24, 1979, issue of *Family Health* revealed that a protein substance known as Interferon, which is normally programmed to fend off viruses, can turn against the body's tissues and worsen the course of certain diseases. Certain factors, as yet undetermined, can make this protein substance turn traitor against its host body.

Always interested in medical advances, Francie said that it would soon be discovered that a mere drop of one's blood can provide all the data necessary to complete physical analysis.

The winter issue, 1979, *Science Digest* told of a new process called, "electropharesies," which can now establish one's sex, state of health, and ethnic background by a single drop of blood.

For some time in the course of her prophetic attunement, Francie foresaw the development of a solar battery for automobiles.

In January 1980, newspapers carried the word that such a battery might well be on its way toward a practical reality. A Chinese wire service announced that a solar-powered pleasure boat, noiseless and pollution free and capable of carrying five or six people, had begun service on a scenic lake in a South China province. The top of the pleasure boat is constructed of 3,168 small monocrystalline silicon cells, which collect energy from the sun and generate 120 watts of power. The battery can hold enough power to drive the electric motor for three hours.

Elsewhere in this book, we shall detail Francie's predictions for the next twenty years and into the new century, but in the remainder of this chapter, we wish to demonstrate that psychic abilities and other special gifts are common among the Star People.

Toni A., Boston, Massachusetts, hears a very strong "buzzing" sound which announces psychic events before they enter her reality. When she was eleven, she saw a next-door neighbor who had died. She not only spoke to him, but she packed up her clothes so that she might accompany him for a way.

"I knew that death was not the end of people," Toni said. "And I knew that I had an ability to see and to hear things that others could not." For a time, Toni thought that she should enter a convent and find comfort in a religious order.

Toni keeps in touch with her guidance through automatic writing.

"When I sit at the typewriter and say, 'Okay,' a thought transference will come through me. It seems like a 'higher me' talking, but some choices of words don't sound like my way of speaking."

Sometimes Toni's lesson plans (she is a teacher) will come through in perfect order. In dreams, the characters provide her with messages directly in context with her life. On waking, she may hear words or songs which answer her questions. On other occasions, a sentence will be "boomed" through her consciousness.

Richard B. of Broomfield, Colorado, also hears the symptomatic Star People buzzing sound preceding the solution to a perplexing problem.

"Sometimes," he observes, "it is related to an interesting idea that had not occurred to me previously."

Richard, although not an engineer by educational requirements, has perplexed many experts with his ability to design and to build complex machines for industrial production. He has a creative nature of a high degree, together with the knack of envisioning the mechanics of a device and of predicting how it will work. Without any sort of extensive mathematical calculations, Richard has often proposed concepts which an engineer decreed would not work—only to prove to the surprise of the experts that it did.

As a child, Richard felt that living with his parents was a temporary condition, that he belonged somewhere else.

In high school, he was considered a "mad inventor" because of his ability to analyze things and to ascertain quickly their nature and function. In the face of ridicule from his peers, he learned to suppress his "far-out ideas."

For a time, Richard became a loner, but he emerged in later life as a person who was knowledgeable, even a bit outspoken, on a number of areas of expertise.

Although she is now a twenty-five-year-old housewife and mother of two children, Mrs. Diane C. of Tulane, California, remembers vividly the night her father died, as she, a thirteen-year-old, lay dreaming of the fatal accident in the most minute details. The automobile collision occurred over fifteen miles away, but Diane "heard" the crash.

"I was there beside my father," Diane remembered. "My grandmother thought it was just a bad dream when I woke up and became hysterical. I told her that my father had been in an accident, that the police were trying to cut him out. I could actually hear the sirens, and I could see everything that was happening.

"The next day, a telephone call told Grandmother that I had been telling the truth.

"My father had died on the freeway, just as I said he had. Later, when she read about the accident in the newspaper, she saw that I had seen every detail.

"A few years later, I had a dream about my Uncle Willie, whom I had only met once when I was a little girl. I told Grandmother that he was going to be killed. I told her how it would happen and who would kill Uncle Willie. She received word of his death a few days later. Everything was just as I said it would be.

"My grandmother is very religious. She said my abilities were 'of the Devil.' She hauled me down to our pastor, who told her that I had ESP, powers that God had given me, but he didn't encourage me to use them!

"But then when I read about your work with the Star People, I thought, 'That's me! That's why I felt I never belonged. I'm a Star Person. I have most of the characteristics you listed."

Suleiman C.E. of Los Angeles is another who has a good number of the Star People characteristics. When he was five years old and suffering from a severe cold, Light Beings took him from his bed and transported him to a circular room. Here they placed him on a table and told him to go to sleep. The voice was strong and kind, Suleiman remembers, and when he awakened, he was in his bedroom and completely well. "And I have remained so for thirty-four years," he commented.

When he was six, a neighborhood bully pointed a BB

gun directly at Suleiman's eye at very close range and pulled the trigger. "I saw the BB emerge from the barrel, slowly rolling in the air. I moved out of the way and let it hit the tree behind me. The cruel boy was terrified and ran inside his house."

Suleiman has maintained a regular contact with the Light Beings and with what he believes to be extraterrestrials. He, too, hears a buzzing sound preceding his involvement in psychic activity.

Lindsay T. of Weyburn, Saskatchewan, Canada, received her activating experience with an angel or a Light Being when she was about eight years old. The episode was so profoundly moving for the young girl that she believed she should become a missionary. Although such was not to be her path, she did become a deeply religious child.

"Up to the age of fifteen, I was able to practice and control telepathy," Lindsay told us. "Very frequently, I was able to foretell events as well.

"Once when my mother went for a holiday in British Columbia, I told my father that she would bring me an ivory letter opener as a gift. This was a most unusual gift for a ten-year-old, and it was not something that I desired. When mother arrived home with the knife, it sparked some lively discussion, you can be sure."

Now in her mid-thirties, Lindsay revealed that her daughter has an almost photographic memory and has regular ESP experiences. Her son began speaking at only seven months and continues to give evidence of a high I.Q. Once again, it seems that Star People beget Star Children.

When Martha S. of Phoenix, Arizona, was five years old, the spirit of her grandmother visited her and explained that she was leaving. When Martha was taken to the funeral some days later, she decided that everyone was crying because they were being left behind while grandmother got to go to Heaven.

Martha has been receiving the "Star People" buzz in her ears preceding a psychic event for many years now. By the time she was eleven, she was having trouble with doors and cupboards opening and objects falling—when no one was near them.

Her hearing developed to an abnormal pitch so that she was able to "hear" electricity.

She discovered that she could "think at" animals and insects and that by concentration she could get people and animals to do as she wished.

She awakened several times during this period to find someone, or something, holding her hand while she slept. She excelled at ESP games, and she had a number of out-of-body experiences.

Recently, Martha was awakened by a ringing sound to perceive a golden figure standing very close to her bedside. The figure began to glow, and it remained near Martha for at least five minutes.

The golden figure has, at the time of her report, visited Martha on four occasions, each time leaving her with a feeling of peace and calm.

"All have been given access to special gifts so that they might affect positively the environment and all those within it," Francie has been told. "Beyond the normal five senses, we possess the ability to know of things outside of our present reality. Due to a subliminal, connecting undercurrent, intelligences outside of our physical dimension are reachable.

"Through meditation and various disciplines, we can alter our reality and transcend into a greater reality, attuning ourselves with abilities inherent to that level of awareness. It is this transcendence beyond ourselves and our dimension that causes us to be as gods. Through such transcendence, we find the ability to perform acts considered miraculous in our physical, Earth-plane reality, *i.e.*, healing, communicating with angelic beings, returning balance to a lifeform by absolving the chaos or negativity within, prophesying, affecting matter, and seeing events occur at great distances.

"All of these feats are possible when one learns the way to transcend into a higher vibrational reality where these abilities are commonplace. Yet all these abilities are but manifestations of the Source. We are always connected to the undercurrent of Life that emerges in various realities. From the moment of our birth, we, being multidimensional, possess contact with our Soul, our spirit, and our body, and we are all capable of 'miraculous' feats. We are four-dimensional beings in a three-dimensional reality.

"Meditating on any object, be it a candle flame, a beam of sunlight, or a grain of sand can pierce the dimensions that divide us. Meditation can lift the veil of darkness which shrouds our world of denser vibrations and enable us to find the true reality of all things.

"The Star People have several gifts available to them from the undercurrent of Life. They can more easily transcend Earth plane reality because of their genetic inheritance from the Sowers.

"The Starseed can determine what gifts they are to emphasize, which abilities will more ably assist them in their mission, by practicing meditation. The discussion of various meditative techniques, which have been outlined in previous chapters, will greatly assist both Starseed and Star Helper in realizing the special gift that they are to develop and the special mission which they are to accomplish."

Chapter Seventeen: Rearing the Star Child

Our society is one in which we tend to raise our children by the standards in vogue. We attempt to, and do, pattern our children by the general disciplinary attitude that currently governs our society.

There were times when it was commonly accepted that a child should be seen and not heard. Children were not permitted to speak their views, were overworked, and dared not voice an objection. Discipline was extremely harsh, and "strappings" were common. Fathers "boxed" their son's ears, and mothers dared not interfere with what they felt were the necessary measures needed to gain the desired results of obedience from their children. During those times a child could not wait to be released as an adult.

As a pendulum extends its span from one extreme point to another, a period of almost no discipline followed. Children were permitted not only to voice their opinions, but were heard expressing their objections by screaming in total protest to the parent's

This chapter is excerpted in part from Francie's *Reflections From an Angel's Eye.*

wishes and doing as they pleased. Parents became almost victimized, and many mothers were reduced to tears, at their wit's-end, trying to control the actions of their children.

These two extremes are behind us; we are now approaching a middleground.

A realization has been reached by most parents that a child should be permitted to express his feelings, but still maintain the due respect for the parent's views. Parents realize that guidelines must be given and that the child should be made aware of the love that is available as progress is gained through the learning period.

One wonders, Where do I begin? How best do I guide my child? What manner of teaching should I employ? From what should I glean my wisdom so as to provide a fertile, consistent guideline for my child to follow?

I want our child to be unhampered in his own realization of life, capable of conversing and expanding his concepts and knowledge, yet respectful and compassionate in his interrelationships with others.

A New Age is dawning throughout the entire world, as a new seedling emerges. A new generation will live, love, and grow. Your role as a parent is of utmost importance. Now more than ever before, you must observe the guiding light that ushers in the Star Child.

The Mother cried from Creation's pain, "He's mine, all mine! From my body he came." And God spoke,

> " 'Tis but a fragment of life
> A part of the whole
> To you, your child.
> To me, a Soul!"

YOUR CHILD'S SOUL

A full realization of the Soul and its purpose should be attained before one begins to rear the Star Child.

There are many ways through which you might gain such a realization, but the most thorough and true way is through meditation.

In meditating on the Soul of your child, knowledge of its true origin, purpose, and desire will be given to you. You will then realize that a great responsibility will soon be yours.

Your child is not truly yours, but belongs to the universe. All souls belong to the Heavenly Realm of the Source—God—and as the parent, we are but the Soul-chosen guide. We must show the child the way, so that the Soul may receive lessons in living, loving, and understanding in order to affect its return to the domain from whence it came.

It is clearly stated in Ezekiel 18:4: "Behold, all Souls are mine. . . ." This declaration must be remembered by the parent at all times. When such a realization is attained, the rearing of the Star Child will become a joy that will not be surpassed by any other accomplishment.

It is only because of ignorance that we hinder a child in attaining the truths to be learned. In ignorance, we violate our children and thwart their learning processes.

Man knows not the ways of God. Through his lack of knowledge he fears all that he cannot understand. He fears the continual changes that are evident throughout his life. The freedom of his childhood passes; the pets he cherished die; his childhood friends disperse; he eventually suffers the loss of his parents; and he watches with sorrow the passing of his youth.

All of these painful events cause him to desire permanency, and he begins clinging to all around him—his family, his children, society, position, social tradition—for he is afraid. He attempts to control his surroundings in order to achieve a feeling of stability. Since permanence is an impossible desire to fulfill, frustration and unhappiness result. Frustration kindles the fire of anger and hatred. This anger is vented toward all he cannot control.

Many parents seek to control their child—commanding, demanding, instilling fear, ceasing their child's true function as a being, a being inhabited by a Soul—a Soul that must learn to relate to others, loving and growing in the knowledge of all things.

An unenlightened parent cannot properly guide the Star Child, nor can he fulfill his own Soul's purpose. We must never desire to control our child, but merely to guide, teach, and create an awareness of the reason for all life's existence on Earth. In so doing, the physical life of that child will be enriched, and he will realize happiness while attaining his goal on the spiritual plane.

Think then in this way: There will exist in my home a being whose Soul descended from Heaven. This Soul, in its desire to return, has chosen to inhabit the body of the babe being born unto me. It has chosen this very family and home for its learning process, and I shall always endeavor to help it attain all that it must learn to gain the awareness necessary for its return to the Highest Vibration—the Source.

The full realization that one is to begin working with a Soul is essential. A person being born to you must be guided, tended, cared for, and loved. An awesome responsibility has been entrusted to you. Your child is not solely yours, but is a part of the whole universe.

PREPARATION

It would be much better if awareness could be reached by the mother and father *before* the child is born. The mother, while carrying the child, should make preparations for its emergence. The father, while preparing for the child, should examine carefully his responsibility in the family unit.

You must produce and make ready the future's love child. Your child should be so filled with love and understanding that those emotions emanate from his very being.

We are all aware of the sensitivity of babies as to their surroundings. Their keen sense of awareness, of hearing, touching, and seeing far surpasses that of an adult. The slamming of a door will cause most babies to burst into tears. Mothers are well aware of the efforts they must employ in trying to place a sleeping babe in its crib and tiptoe from the room so as not to awaken it.

Your baby is totally dependent upon its senses. As we mature, our senses become more calloused as they are bombarded by the environment. Yet, we can still be influenced by various stimuli, such as music, colors, sounds of hatred and sounds of love.

Music plays an important part in setting moods. It may stimulate one to action, cause one to think, or bring soothing sleep. Loud bass music can be felt as well as heard. Sitting too close to an amplifier pounding out a deep bass rhythm can cause one to *feel* the very vibration itself. All of us have heard of the shattering of a glass by an opera singer. Ultrasound as a weapon is no longer a fantasy of Buck Rogers. Therefore, one should realize that a child's nervous system should not undergo the shock and strain of loud, harsh music, but should be soothed and calmed by the symphonic strings of an orchestra. Be alert to the fact that shock is what you wish to avoid if harmony and balance are to govern his system.

The effect of colors on man is well-recognized. We use colors to emphasize our moods. Bright colors show forth in splendor at our fairs and carnivals, and the somberness of black sobers our funerals. Do you think this is merely by the dictates of society, or do *you* feel more alive and alert around bright colors? Do certain colors irritate or calm you?

Various tests have been conducted all over the world that show that men and women can feel colors through their fingertips. Be they people who are blindfolded, it has been noted colors can be felt. Those who are blind, having never seen colors, speak of the color we know as "red" causing a tingling sensation, "blue" being cool, "orange" being warm, and so on. Our hospitals have chosen the calm color of green as the predominant color of decor. The warning signs that govern our traffic control are either bright red or bright yellow to gain our attention.

A wise mother chooses the "calm" colors for her child's room, as well as his or her clothing. Red is stimulating and increases tension; yellow is cheerful; green, refreshing; blue, cool. Violet is perhaps the best color for the New Age child, as it provides the vibrations that harmonize with a balanced personality.

With an energetic child, it is also helpful to eliminate bright loud colors, harsh music, noisy toys, all food coloring from his diet, and flourescent lighting from areas he/she frequents. All objects in the child's room should be selected with care. Toys should be chosen that stimulate, educate, and emanate love. No toys should be given that are of the destructive nature, such as rubber knives, guns, and the like. Soft dolls and teddy bears should be given to the child, whether it is a boy or a girl. Do we not want our sons to be able to care for and show love to their children, just as we do our daughters? All toys should be introduced to the child by a loving parent, who should take time to show the child the proper way to play with the toy.

I have found that star-shaped, luminous decals are excellent for decorating a child's ceiling. They are nearly invisible by day, but they glow beautifully by night. In a darkened room, as the child is preparing to sleep, the decals appear to twinkle as if they comprise a starry sky over his head. Instead of a ceiling, your child is provided with a simulation of natural beauty, the handiwork of the Source.

The glowing stars also serve to attract the eye of the child with delight, preventing him from noticing darkened corners and shadows that may frighten him. If you wish, you may place the stars on the ceiling in scattered outlines of the Big and Little Dippers and various zodiacal signs, as a form of teaching. Such formations can be found pictured in atlases and in books on astronomy.

Love cannot be over-emphasized in raising the Star Child. It is the lack of love that kindles the fire of resentment and hatred, thereby blocking the flow of concern and compassion for our fellow man.

There should exist at all times the sound of love in the parent's voice—a soothing quality that says, "You're very important to me and I love you very much," even if one is merely saying "Hi!" In this way the child becomes so accustomed to that sound and the continual flow of love that he or she becomes shocked and filled with anxiety the moment it is withdrawn.

It is the withdrawal of the sound of love that provides the only weapon necessary in disciplining a wayward child.

The facial expression worn by the parent as he or she enters a child's room is also important. Even if the mother is weary or ill, she should muster a smile for that child, as should the father who comes home at the end of a hard day's work.

Throughout the child's life, a smile should always greet him or her, and may sometimes be accompanied by a raised eyebrow as if to say: "I notice your presence and I am pleased." Obviously, a frown toward a disobedient child or a child about to disobey, will carry far more weight than if it is used by a parent who continuously frowns.

After the child has ceased the action that brought about the necessary discipline, a flow of love should return within a few minutes. A look of approval should be seen on the face of the parent, and the sound of love should return to the voice. This is all that is ever needed when correcting a child in public.

When in private, a child should be taken to another room, and the reason for his or her discipline should be given. It should be completely explained, and the child's understanding should be explored. The "whys" of a child should always be answered, lovingly.

After the explanation and an understanding has been reached, the child should be held and shown love before being returned to the room where the discipline became necessary. As was stated before, *never* embarrass your child in public. No purpose is served, but an undermining of your relationship with your child can begin.

Threatening is totally uncalled for and is employed by an immature parent who cannot handle the situation. If you have become so upset that you have taken out the frustrations on your child, show genuine sorrow and explain that you realize you acted in a foolish manner and promise you will try never to violate the child again.

It is a very good practice for the parent to point out to the child the poor behavior patterns used by other adults and children. This can be accomplished when the parent and child go about their daily routines together, such as shopping.

When your child sees a parent bullying his or her child or a child slapping his younger brother or sister, you should choose this time to inject many teachings and thoughts of awareness in your child. This can be accomplished by asking various questions, such as, "What is that mother doing that is wrong for her child?" or "Why do you think he is slapping his brother so?"

A child that has been made aware of the beauty of love will answer, "Because they are unhappy and do not know real love for one another. They are taking out their angers and frustrations on one who cannot defend himself."

Then, ask your child further, "What does that do to the little one?"

"It teaches more hatred to pass on to others," he will answer.

On and on it continues, and the many situations you encounter as you share your lives become your living classroom. Always keep in mind that your child, observing an angry, bitter parent, has lost much respect for that parent or has been guided the wrong way when observing the parent display a false behavior when approached by an acquaintance. Watching the parent feign a sickeningly sweet manner, listening to him or her pretend an assumed joy, and observing as the disposition of the parent immediately returns to its previously held anger, will teach a child subterfuge . . . or even worse, to have a deceitful manner.

Even more damaging to the child is to observe a parent fawning over a woman and then hear the parent make a disparaging remark as she departs. Can the child trust such a parent when he has just observed her dual personality?

Your child will either imitate your ways and become your living mirror, or he will rebel and vow never to be like you when he matures. Which would you prefer?

It is of utmost value on many levels to raise your child with the belief in a God-Creator-Father and a God-Creator-Mother who unconditionally love him or her and will do so even after death. That no matter what the child may do or wherever they may go in life, their Heavenly Father and Mother will forever love and care for them.

This belief will sustain your child in the total balance of True Love, when you falter or fail in your raising of him. For we ourselves cannot be perfect. We, too, are trying to overcome the imperfections in our own rearing.

One should emphasize that they are merely the *Earth* parents and that the child should pattern himself after the Heavenly Parent, rather than duplicating our errors. Teaching the child the perfections of the Heavenly Parent, the balance of love given universally to all people, the compassion for humankind, the forgiveness of sin, etc., will offer a better guideline for the child to pattern himself, a higher goal to attain. Needless to say, the parent on Earth, who is daily observed by the child, *will* carry the most weight in the child's patterning, but a higher code of proper conduct has been set.

This teaching of a Heavenly Father and a Heavenly Mother as loving creators is helpful in many ways. The security and perfections of the unconditional love vibration that exist in the Heavenly Realm will provide a firm foundation when all else fails in his or her life.

The New Testament of the Bible provides many such loving lessons. One need not be a Christian to benefit from these wise teachings.

TALES TO TEACH BY

Go not by Mother Goose you see, for teachings are what needs to be;
Her tales of woe and rhyme tell naught of life's battles that must be fought.
'Tis not bare cupboards, mice with chopped tails, and sheep that are sought
o'er mountains and dales
That teach your children what they should know, for seeds of love must
they learn to sow.
But stories of those who fare not well when cruel to others you must tell;
Of God's justice that gives to man
All he has wrought by his own hand.
Let these tales be woven of gossamer lace
With Knights and Dragons that meet face to face;
Many lessons of love must be there, too,
To remain in their hearts their whole life through.

When the child is of an understanding age, you should create stories which contain within them the lessons you are trying to convey. These stories should always show the importance of love and the reasons for truth. They should seek to demonstrate why control is necessary to achieve the desired results in life.

HOW TO WEAVE A TEACHING TALE

Make a mental note of the child's principal acts of disobedience or disrespect which were shown that day. Prepare to weave a bedtime tale around such acts in order to teach your child why such actions are undesireable.

Bedtime is an especially good time for such a lesson, as the child has been bathed, made comfortable, and relaxed. He or she is also weary from the day's activities, and he or she will have few distractions from his teaching time.

Say, for example, that your child balked aloud when you wished to clothe him or her in particular attire, that he or she created a scene of disobedience in front of others, and that your child refused to eat an item of nutritional food. The teaching tale that you weave should be centered around an angry, non-complying child.

It may be a good idea to choose the opposite sex for your story-child, so that your child will not feel that his or her actions of the day are being attacked. Such an early realization would place your child on the defensive, thereby blocking an effective learning of the important lesson.

You might also wish to place your central character in a completely different environment, such as a castle, a foreign country, another planet. The story-child, therefore, may be a prince or princess, an animal, or an alien child.

Care must be taken in disguising the character of your child, as well as the lesson to be taught, so that you will not make your child unduly suspicious of your motives in relating the bedtime tale. The exact act of disobedience that your child displayed should never be used;

rather, a similar act should be chosen for the story.

For illustration, if your child shoved his plate of un-desired food away from him until it fell from the table, your story-child should be shown throwing an unwanted object at the person who gave it to him.

The basic steps which one should follow in weaving a teaching tale are: 1) Exaggerating the circumstances which portray the wrong action; 2) Relating dire cir-cumstances which result from such actions, together with the misery caused and felt by such actions; 3) Exaggerating the attitude assumed that shows disobedience; 4) The display of great sorrow by the story-child as forgiveness is begged and promises are given to repent; 5) The understanding, forgiveness, and compassion shown by those around the story-child; 6) How the story-child totally changed from such poor behavior and how happy all those around him became; and 7) How happy the story-child was forever more because of his behavior change.

I cannot emphasize enough that you must spend great amounts of time with your child. At least one or two hours a day should be devoted to a totally uninterrupted oasis of time with your child. There should be no telephone calls, no visits from friends. Both your friends and his should know this time belongs to your child.

Many things can be accomplished during this time. I have found that the first hour is best spent studying the anatomy of the human body, learning every minute part—such as the eye and its wonders, the ear and how sound is sensed and heard. Eventually the sex organs and their function will be the topic, together with birth and its beautiful process.

Each child should have a pencil and pad on which to draw and jot notes, and then a test should be given. Praise the child and show your love, not only when he gets an answer correct, but even if he errs.

The next hour should be devoted to proper behavior,

problems which occur in relating to others, and so forth. The child should be permitted to pour out his feelings on every subject.

This is also a good time for you to recall some of the problems you experienced as a child, for by so doing, your child will see that you have had similar feelings and have endured similar problems. Such a rapport will indicate to your child that you can better understand his/her daily trials and tribulations.

After this period of talk, there should follow a time of play. Wrestling, tickling, kissing, and plenty of physical fondling should be employed here. Enjoy your New Age child.

Always remember that when the two of you watch television, movies, or listen to music, you can always be touching in some manner. It may be merely tapping your child's shoulder or lightly stroking back a wisp of hair. Rubbing his back or massaging his feet will provide him with a relaxed feeling in which he will easily be able to receive love.

If one parent is immature and fails to provide these lessons of love, the other parent must compensate for the failing of the immature one. It is best the mature parent seek a substitute parent, such as a loving grandmother to compensate for an immature mother or a loving grandfather to compensate for an immature father. If this is not possible, talk often of the mature loving ways of their Heavenly Father and Mother, who love them deeply, will guard over them, and try to help them in every way. This will provide the balance necessary for the child so that he will learn to love more completely.

It serves no useful purpose in the ultimate end for the mature parent to side with the immature parent merely to present a unified front to the child. For to whom will the child be able to turn? It is better the child have one mature parent than none.

*   *   *

GUIDANCE FROM THE STARS

There have been a number of books written on astrology and children. Keep an open mind and explore the possibilities that such an ancient science might truly be able to offer you yet another means of discovering a deeper understanding of your child. It has always impressed me how uncannily accurate the *personality* traits indicated by the zodiac seem to be as I interact with Star Children. A little poem I wrote indicates the zodiacal traits of the

"Signs on High"

Forceful Arians with a confident stride;
Practical Taureans in whom you can confide;
Energetic Geminians with loving chatter;
Quiet Cancerians, pretending slights never matter;
The leadership of Leo, tempered with understanding;
Shy, firm Virgoans, who rarely are demanding;
The love of Librans, ever balancing a decision;
The conviction of the Scorpio, known for their precision;
Jovial Sagittarians with a loving manner;
Persevering Capricorns, determination their banner;
Idealistic Aquarians, being helpful is their goal;
Dreamy Pisceans, creative in their role.
All these are in the Heavens and sprinkled
O'er the Earth;
Soul-chosen in their purpose and evident
from birth.

Chapter Eighteen: Blood on the Moon: Earth Changes and Cataclysms

So many of the Star People have been told that humankind is entering a new cycle of evolution which will be designed primarily to enable the species more completely to become fourth-dimensional beings on a much higher spiritual vibration.

According to channelled information, on few other planets in the universe did humankind fall so firmly in the third-dimensional plane of physical existence than it did on Earth. The conditions that lock humankind so completely into time and space have made of Earth an excellent "schoolroom" by which to learn and to gain experiences in the basic lessons of life. But now an important cycle is drawing to a close, and it is time for humankind to raise its spiritual consciousness.

Star Person Robin McPherson (now Nicholas) of the Light Affiliates, Yale, British Columbia, channelled the following message from Higher Intelligence:

There is a whole new world waiting for you, people of Earth.

The fourth dimension is one of subtleness, of light

shades of beauty. With your increased vibrations, you will be able to see this subtleness with an intensity beyond your imagining. The rocks, the flowers, the greenery, the very earth on which you stand will be stepped up in frequency to match this dimensional vibration, and each form of life will take on new shades of being. . . .

Life is interdimensional, and so is man. But man has lost consciousness of his true perfection.

Learn to flow with these dimensional frequencies and learn to become flexible.

Do not allow yourself to become crystallized, for each man has a shattering point if he continues to resist the flow of dimensional evolution.

Each man must come to know where he is going and learn to be one with this great dimensional flow. You must shed your old dimension, because you no longer need it.

People of Earth, you are becoming fourth dimensional whether you are ready or not. Leave the old to those who cling to the old. Don't let the New Age leave you behind!

Channel Aleuti Francesca was also informed that the time ahead, which some people call Armageddon, the final conflict between the forces of light and the forces of darkness prior to a Judgment Day, is not to be considered the ending of a planet. Rather, we are all about to witness the ending of a cycle.

The Intelligence who speaks through Aleuti stated that conflicting energy patterns are bombarding Earth at the present time, the chief of which manifest from the "greater inflowing of energies from the Central Sun":

For as these energies are absorbed into the "vehicle," into the molecular, cellular structure of every individual upon your planet, they are then utilized in varying degrees.

The Light-enfilled individual utilizes these energies for his greater ongoing and upliftment in Light.

The individual who is materialistic, who has no concept of a Creator or of forces beyond the physical material energies, finds that these high-frequency energies set up friction within the "body" physical, the "body" emotional, and the "body" mental.

The resistance which is set up to these high-energy sources develops a great degree of discomfort and disease within the individual. Patterns of violence and group violence in your own country, in your universities, and in your cities, are brought about by these high-energy sources and the resistance with which they are met by the materialistic man or woman of Earth.

Each man and woman is seeking and finding, at this time, his or her own level of Soul growth. Each must find his level, and in finding it, establish his own point within a destined pattern. All the Earth's peoples choose now, at the time of decision, between Light and Dark, and rise rapidly in consciousness and in frequency of cellular structure—or they fall into a greater grossness of materialism and density than has heretofore been known.

A great pattern of density awaits the Children of Light on planet Earth. Many physical tests have been given to those who will work with the Lighted ones—those whom you term the Masters of wisdom, who dwell in bodies non-physical, and those of ourselves, who come to you and will come in increasing numbers from Space. Many times these tests are subtle in nature and are not at the time realized for that which, in reality, they are. Yet at each test which is passed, a greater discernment and discrimination is evidenced, acted upon, and that Soul unfolds in Light substance and moves onward.

We send, at this time, much energy of Light, much love; for the scene on Earth planet is not one of harmony, as viewed from our perspective, but one of great difficulty. Yet the Souls who move forward and onward and upward have conquered greatly and have achieved to a point of evolution. . . .

We say once more: The Earth is a training school for gods.

Look within to your own godhead; discover it; express it; and Be the being created of the One Creator: god and goddess in essence, aspiring to the Light Eternal.

*   *   *

Certain channellers have predicted that a most dramatic cycle is about to reoccur which would set into motion an axis-shift for the planet. According to serious-minded researchers who have looked into the matter, an axis-shift seems to take place approximately every 9,000 years. When this tilt occurs, what was frozen often becomes tropical, and that which is in the temperate zones may become part of an arctic wasteland. An axis tilt, many say, is overdue and could take place anytime before the year 2000.

Francie has said repeatedly that her guide has told her that we, the people living today, are in a particular age when several major events will occur that will radically and drastically change not only our life styles but the surface of Earth.

"These cataclysmic events will occur, not because mankind has been wicked and sinful and must now receive collective punishment, but because of certain cyclic events which shape our planet's geological and vibrational structure. In the approaching cycle, the polarities will reverse, and all matter on Earth will rise to a higher vibrational frequency.

"No single member of humankind lives long enough to observe these cycles, but from the viewpoint of the cosmic intelligences, all major occurrences come in cycles. All matter is energy, and energy comes to us in waves.

"We will experience the birth throes of the New Age for approximately twenty more years, wherein there will exist earthquakes and floodings, with their terrible shadows of famine and pestilence. As conditions stand today, the channellings have indicated that the New Age will occur in 1999, but because its advent is due to an accumulation of polarized electromagnetic energies, the precise time is not yet determined."

On May 22, 1979, Francie and I were enroute to San

Juan, Puerto Rico, where we had been invited to participate in a seminar on parapsychology. During the flight from New York to the islands, Francie received a teaching-vision which instructed her to warn those people who lived in coastal areas that those locations would become dangerous during the approaching time of transition.

After she had clarified the vision in her mind, Francie spoke distinctly: "Those who live on the coastal regions of all countries will be in danger during the time of transition, which will accelerate in the 1980s.

"The entire Earth will experience many disasters—quakes, floodings, splittings, and famine. An inner shift of energies, of polarities, will occur, shaking our very foundation. Those who seek to live by the Spirit must be strong in the years which lie ahead. All will be affected by these many catastrophes in varying degrees."

It has been shown to Francie that thoughts and actions are vibrational in nature. Since they are magnetically governed, they are attracted to either the positive or negative poles of Earth. Here, they accumulate, until they reach such a degree of intensity that the tension affects weakened areas which normally exist in the Earth's crust. Because these accumulated vibrations affect all of matter, the mounting tensions will cause these weakened areas to become high-risk places.

Francie's vision of the time of Earth Changes and cataclysms took the form of a great three-pronged split that extended down from the north polar region:

"In the manner of a three-taloned claw, this will gravely affect the Earth's crust and will cause considerable devastation. This three-taloned claw will encompass half of the world, and will indicate areas of great tension and stress.

"The first talon will cross diagonally downward over the eastern region of the Soviet Union, then lower into eastern China.

"The second talon will stretch diagonally downward across central Canada and into mid-California.

"The third talon will cross central Greenland, from northwest to east, move downward into the Mediterranean and into Northern Africa.

"These are the paths of the three-taloned claw. These are the places where major tensions will exist during the coming electromagnetic shifting of the polar regions.

"Areas on either side of the three gripping talons will be affected, but all land near the coastal regions will suffer to an even greater degree with quakes, floods, great winds, and climatical changes. Those areas farther inland will be the least afflicted.

"The time of great devastation has occurred on Earth twice before. On the first occasion, there were only animals on the planet. On the second occasion, people suffered the catastrophes, and many earlier cultures and civilizations were destroyed.

"These great devastations are vibrational, accumulative events which are natural to this planet. No one knows the exact time the fast-approaching devastation will begin, but it will be soon, quite likely before 1999."

Francie was told that in order to discover the "safe" places during the coming cataclysms, one must first "feel" and meditate upon those areas which are the strongest. When choosing a place to live, one must select a solid area that can withstand great strain.

"Feel those areas which emanate the *least* vibrations," Francie advised. "Study the topography of all regions and ascertain those which are the driest. Areas near bodies of water of any major proportion are in danger. Water in vast amounts will shift, take different courses, different directions, and be jarred from present boundaries. The amount of miles inland which will be considered a safe area will depend upon the size of the body of water it is near.

"Even in the driest of areas, far from water, the present emanations existing suggest splittings, shiftings, settlings, and major cave-ins. These ground shifts will occur not only in regions near the three-pronged strain, but in particular areas that were once seabeds, where underground caverns now exist. These regions will not be able to withstand the shakings, the shiftings, and the strain.

"The safest regions primarily will be the desert regions—as long as one takes into consideration those areas which are presently desert, but are dangerous due to their proximity to large bodies of water.

"The following, then, are the *safest* areas: major parts of Arizona; the southern part of Colorado, the large, western area of New Mexico, and the northern region of Mexico. Inland Australia is safe, as is mid-Arabia, the southwest Soviet Union, and the driest region of northwest China.

"You, who are Star People, permit your 'mark on the forehead,' the so-called 'third eye,' to lead you to safety. As you keep in mind the regions above, meditate upon the area of thought that feels safe to you. You are aware that the dangerous emanations and regions do exist. Your inner guidance will help you make your final decision in ascertaining your safest place.

"All people of Spirit must be ready to share their energies during this time of travail. The Star People's capacity to love will be greater during this time, as they observe the birth throes of a New World of higher vibrational frequencies.

"Love must be the guiding force in all that we undertake," Francie concluded. "The next two decades will be among the most important that humankind has ever faced. The entire species is about to face its moment of decision."

Chapter Nineteen: The Meaning of Armageddon

Christianity has portrayed the destiny of humankind as steadily unfolding according to a great plan of God.

Apocalyptic thought presupposes a universal history in which the Divine Author of that pageant will reveal and manifest His strength, His glory, and His secrets in a dramatic End-Time that will, with ultimate finality, establish the God of Israel as the one true God. Armageddon represents one last, climactic struggle between the Forces of Light and the Forces of Darkness.

Humankind seems to have an everlasting penchant toward dualism. There seems to be something within the collective consciousness of the species that requires the portrayal of certain elements in its environment as either good *or* evil.

The Star People appear to be almost totally free of any fears of shadow-lurking demons and world-conquering Anti-Christs. Apocalyptic literature, warning of "666," the Beast, and announcements of a last, bloody, global conflict between good and evil may all be interpreted in a very different manner from that which is currently being so widely preached by Judgment Day-oriented, fundamentalist-inspired writers, motion

179

picture directors, and mass market theologians. The cosmic timetable in the book of Revelation may be viewed as an invitation toward the divine adventure of a new life in a New Age, rather than a passport to doom and damnation. The Star People are very much aware that all about them is evidence that an Old World is dying, but they contemplate with hope the New World that is in the process of being born.

As there exist polarities on the physical plane, so will there be found polarities on the spiritual plane of Earth, Francie was directed to relay during one of her channelling sessions.

The Christian Bible speaks of these polarities which exist in the spiritual realm when it teaches of a God who represents good and His opposite, Satan, who represents evil. Christianity prophesizes a merging of the two planes which will occur during a final battle of good and evil which is called Armageddon.

Christians believe that the final outcome of Armageddon has been foretold. Good will triumph over evil, and Satan, together with his followers, will be kept from influencing humankind forevermore. There will be peace on Earth and good will among men.

Christian thought also envisions a Day of Judgment, when the "sheep" shall be separated from the "goats," when the dead will rise from their graves and will be judged for their deeds and misdeeds on Earth. For many, this will be a day of great mourning, when they will gnash their teeth, faint from fear, and beg the mountains to fall upon them.

The belief that such a holocaust would one day come to pass, together with a Judgment Day that would involve each and every Soul, intrigued Francie from a very early age. She decided, as do so many Christians, that to be on the side of the "sheep" would be her lifelong goal. She achieved a vague kind of comfort from the fact that her French surname actually meant "Easter Lamb" or "Passover Lamb."

As Francie grew older, the approaching event of Armageddon caused many questions to come to mind.

She wanted to know where the spirits went when they died. If no spirits went to Heaven or Hell until the Judgment Day, were they just lying dormant somewhere until after Armageddon had been fought?

If God and Satan were going to fight it out with all their attendant hosts of Angels and Demons somewhere in the spiritual realm, why did generations of physical bodies have to be reassembled and brought back into being just to be judged?

When she asked her guide, Kihief, to explain Armageddon to her, Francie received the following reply: "The polarities which exist on the Earth-plane create the various vibrations which permit learning. Whether an individual does or does not choose to do a particular act, there is learning inherent in the very process of choice."

"Earth Beings are surrounded by many 'theories' regarding the 'good' and the 'evil,' and all these ideas are intellectualized until mass confusion exists," the channel Illiana wrote in her journal, *New Age Teachings*. According to Illiana's view:

> Those who seek only intellectual understanding have not risen above the Third Dimension of Consciousness, so nothing that you say can really aid them in understanding. They are still in need of experiencing the "dual" principles until a time arrives when they "sense" the complete purpose behind this basic Law and its value to your Soul-evolvement.
>
> You, who transcend the Third-Dimensional state and dwell spiritually and mentally on a Fourth Dimension, fully comprehend the principle of Life, that which is thought of as the "good and evil." Since you understand this principle of balance you are able to put into proper perspective the negative and positive polarities and the validity in this Law operating as it does on planet Earth. To an Earth dweller caught up in the intellectual concepts of a Third-Dimensional world, it is impossible to

explain the Cosmic interpretation of this Basic Law, which raises it into a Spiritual Law of Balance.

To say to the intellectual Earth-mind that ALL is "good" seems simplistic—even trite! Though according to Earth standards these men and women may be intellectual geniuses, they lack the Spiritual Awareness which raises the "human" mind into a Higher Dimension where "good and evil" are simply opposites of the same Principle.

So, my Sons, it is wiser to refrain from "explanations" other than what is easily understood. Rather, strive to impress them, who seek such answers, with the fact that certain spiritual principles *cannot* be adequately defined using words, but that they must be *experienced* by each one.

"All things which exist, whether in our material reality or in the spiritual reality, lead to the Source, for all that is comes from the Source and will eventually return to its point of origin," Francie is convinced.

"The 1960s began the full-scale activation of the Star Person. These inheritors of the New Age began to surface openly during this decade. An old age was dying, and an ancient system, which had existed for millenia, was coming to a close.

"Karma, the Divine Justice, cause and effect, had always existed in equal measure on Earth. In these days, as all matter is transcending to a higher vibration, Karma is being affected as well. The equal measure, the exact balance to the scales of Justice, is being tilted in the favor of Divinity. Therefore, Karma, as we now know it, has been speeded up and is coming to its demise."

The Sixties began the end of the Karmic cycle as all humankind has experienced it, Francie was shown. America is a place where humankind has gathered from the "four corners of Earth." This is a place where all colors, creeds, and nationalities have collected and blended. Therefore, its children will best understand "the sign of the times."

A zero depicts a whole, encompassing all vibrations. If, at the base of a zero (0), we place a straight, upward thrust, we have a "6." Therefore, during the 1960s, all vibrational energy that emanated on Earth went out, away from the planet.

A horizontal line with a sharp, downward thrust forms a "7." Seven indicates that all energy will be leveled off to return immediately and to affect the same lifetime that expended it. The Seventies were years of an accelerated process of learning and awareness. In the past, we had known only of the retribution and learning gained from lifetime to lifetime, "an eye for an eye."

In the Eighties, a new system of the immediate return of vibrations within the same lifetime is being enacted. Karma, as we have known it, has come to a close. Note the movement performed to create an "8." A whole (0) in our denser, physical reality is equaled in form (0) in the spiritual reality, and full balance is caused to exist in an "8." During the Eighties, all of matter, including marriages, corporations, states, principalities, and nations will receive, within its lifetime, in equal measure the vibrations which they send forth. "Instant retribution," you might say.

The Nineties will show the collective whole of the spiritual reality (0) with a straight line of Divine intervention coming down to our lesser vibrational reality, thus forming the "9." The Nineties mark the decade of the beginning of Divine intervention. A new system of Karma, one that will be tilted toward humankind from the Divine, will be instituted. In this new Law of Karma, all good or positive vibrations will best be understood to be returned threefold, for Earth is raising its vibrational reality as all matter returns to the Source. During the Nineties, Divine assistance will come when it will be most sorely needed. This decade will serve as a midwife to bring in the Cosmic Person for the New Age.

Some years ago, I asked Francie to channel information about Armageddon. The following is a compilation of that earlier material and comments and reflections from Francie during the course of our work on this book.

The experience of Earth is for the gathering of three vibrations, unconditional love, wisdom, and knowledge. We all remember an oft-spoken phrase told us during childhood: "Experience is the best teacher."

Though experience is not the only way we learn of a situation, it is the most thorough way we gain true knowledge, wisdom, and the capacity for unconditional love.

Earth is the physical domain where humankind can experience, gain awareness, and become enriched. Through embracing Life in all its pain and glory, we progress forward on the path of awareness toward the Source, God.

The vibrational polarity that exists on the physical plane is the one that governs experience and the learning that accompanies it. This polarity, with its opposing energies, works together to create awareness through experience. All energies that exist on the physical plane have an opposite in exact and equal measure. This Law is also what is commonly known as cause and effect. We reap what we sow. The East Indian word for this Law is Karma.

This Law can best be thought of as an established Divine Justice, for it governs positive, as well as negative, actions; good as well as evil attitudes. All that you do returns to you for the learning, the awareness, the enrichment.

We have been made aware of this governing Law by all of our prophets, Master Teachers, and Saints. The admonition set forth of an "eye for an eye and a tooth for a tooth" clearly explained that on Earth there was a Law of Judgment that was meted out by forces divine. It is also emphasized that this Law was not to be—nor could it have been—governed by man, for even judgmental actions return. "Judge not lest ye be judged," and "Vengeance is mine, not thine."

Our most revered wisemen, our most esteemed religious leaders, have repeatedly warned us of the consequences which would befall us if we defied such a system of polarity and justice. Remember the words of the Master Jesus: "He who kills by the sword shall die by the sword. Whatsoever you do to others will be done to you." These were teachings of divine truths.

As if we were eternal children we have been taught of this law of experience. If we did good acts, we were promised a reward, "Heaven." If we did misdeeds, we were promised a punishment, to be burned in "Hell."

As wise parents give love or punishment to a child in order to guide and instruct him, so did the Higher Beings institute a Pavlovian method consisting of reward and punishment on Earth so that they might better guide and instruct humankind. We must experience Life and the awareness that comes from living it.

Aeons ago, the Starsowers knew well what the reactions of humankind would be if they dared to intervene overtly in Earth understandings. If they would have descended and told all they knew about the proper ways to ascend to the Source, Earthlings, at that primitive stage of development, would have been too stunned by such knowledge.

The wisdom which the Starsowers had acquired had taken thousands of years on their own planet. They were well aware that such wisdom and knowledge could not be learned by the Earthlings in a short span. To reveal all would only have brought forth two unproductive reactions. One would have been the silent shock when a mind has been taxed beyond its limits. The other would have been stark terror, and humankind would have reacted in blind, fear-filled obedience to the divine beings from another world.

Humankind would have learned nothing from either reaction. The Starsowers wished neither to control humankind as robots nor to influence them through fear.

The Starsowers chose to interact with humankind and to begin from our basic understandings. The Starsowers knew that to be most effective they must work within the established order of the existing reality of the Laws of Earth.

The decision was therefore reached which brought about their physical descent to Earth and an interaction with humankind on a physical level. Their intermingling with humankind set in motion a plan of cross-blending, a "seeding," which produced offspring who set about to raise the awareness of humankind. In addition, the genes of the seedlings would carry the knowledge of their starsown heritage, thereby affecting Earth throughout its existence.

The Starsowers, their seeds, and their descendants have given humankind ways of living and rules of conduct—all of which are designed to aid the seeker more positively to gain the many levels of awareness which exist here. Positive energies and actions permit humankind to go forward on the path to the Source. Negative energy, being the opposite, pulls in the opposing direction, causing us either to stand still or to regress on the path.

Awareness is positive, is all, and encompasses the whole. Ignorance is negative, is emptiness, and involves the individual ego. It is the pull between these two energies, these two polarities—Positive, called God; Negative, called Satan—that causes *experience* to exist, to be possible. And with experience comes the learning, the awareness that is Life. No motion is lost, but it is entrapped in the laws of learning, of cause and effect, of Good and Evil.

Humankind's many religious leaders, its philosophers, its prophets have used many metaphors and archetypes in their attempts to depict the Greater Reality so that men and women might be assisted in their understanding on whatever level of awareness they might exist. Therefore, nearly all Earth religions relate a multitude of parables, together with picturesque stories of Angels of Light engaged in physical warfare, sword in hand, against Angels of Darkness. Light (Awareness), we are told, shall always win the final battle.

Depictions of Satan (666) challenging God (999) in a climactic struggle in which God's triumph has already been foretold, means that in this physical world, positive and negative pull within and without us (the battle). Experience permits the awareness (winning). Positive (God) wins, thus enabling us to go forward.

Humankind has been told of this Law in many ways in order to enable us to be more aware, and in the process, to better affect the entire species.

The Starsowers were keenly aware that Earth was involved in the physical reality of polarity struggles. The electrical and magnetic fields of this planet emanate positive and negative energies and pull against themselves. The polarities gather energies unto themselves in such density as to cause a great and a continual straining in the weight of their cumulative division. Often the pull (the battle) becomes so great that the planet nearly divides itself by splitting at the poles.

Although it is unlikely that such a major division would ever occur, as long as physical existence continues, the *experience* of earthquakes, splittings, and floodings will one day culminate in the *winning*, the absorption of a higher energy, newly born. At that time, all things will move forward toward the Highest Energy—the Source.

All that is physical is governed by 1) The Polarities—opposites; 2) The Battle—experience; 3) The Winning—raising of vibrations.

The coming final polarity struggle has been picturesquely described as Armageddon (666, the Beast, versus 999, God; "6" is but a "9" upside down), and even the outcome was accurately foretold. The victory of the positive shall encompass the gaining of a higher vibration, a greater awareness, and a new world for all people—a New Jerusalem.

Chapter Twenty: Star Unions: Inheritors of the New Age

"There are two types of Star People here on Earth who work to aid humankind in attaining awareness," Francie said after a period of reflection.

"The Starseeds are the genetic inheritors of the Sowers. The Star Helpers are evolutionized Earthlings whose 'home' is now in the stars.

"The Star Helpers have achieved their awareness and have progressed beyond other Earthlings, either by inheriting the genes of ancestors who assisted the Star-sowers in their mission or by speeding up their evolutionary development through a disciplined study and a process of initiation. The Star Helpers are as evolved in their awareness as the great mass of Earthlings will be in about a thousand years.

"Both Starseed and Star Helpers are the Star People.

"The sole purpose of existing on Earth is to become enriched with the vibrations inherent in experiencing life and to return with awareness to the Source.

"The Star People wish to assist humankind to discover ways of becoming more enriched, more aware, so that the entire species might accelerate the process of evolutionary growth.''

Raymond P. La C. of British Columbia expressed the understandable reluctance which certain of the Star People have in publicly identifying themselves, but he shared with us a number of relevant details which had accrued from his dialogue with a young Tibetan Lama. "Simply put," Raymond wrote, "the message was as follows":

Beings or inhabitants of Earth are of two main classifications: those who were indigenous to Earth and those who were nonindigenous.

The beings from other parts of the Universe and higher planes of existence eventually entered into a state of catalysis with humanity, marrying the "fair daughters of Earth," and through the laws of genetics, enabling humanity to partake of their own nature (which is something of a mystery). It was as if the "high" and the "low" came into contact so that the level of the "low" could be raised.

The "high" blended its nature with the "low" according to the Divine Plan, so that the "low" could be raised to a higher degree of awareness. The "high ones" became the sacrifices which are often mentioned in Sacred Scriptures, but at the same time, fulfilled their God-given missions.

It has been aptly said that there is never actually a "sacrifice," for the Law of Karma always brings compensation of whatever nature is required. In order to really help, one must "touch" and even become "one" with the one whom one wishes to help. These beings could do no less in order to accelerate man's evolution. Anything less would have been ineffective, and surely God's plan for all his creation must be effective and bear fruit.

What has all this to do with the NOW?

According to the vast cycles relating to man's evolution on Earth, it would seem that a point of time has come when these beings are to come out of their state of catalysis. They are to "externalize" themselves and realize themselves as they once were. We will have what might be called a gathering of the clan—those who once worked together but sort of strayed away from one another to more or less work on their own.

They are feeling stirrings within themselves to return to their former home—wherever that might be. Their task on this Earth, for the most part, is nearly completed. They are therefore to come into their own, as they are of the Starbirth of a distant past. They are the seed of the higher beings who gave in order that God's children may sooner realize their own divinity.

The coming age has been called "The Age of Shambhalla," and it would seem that perhaps another thousand years may be necessary to bring to completion the fulfillment of the age-old mission. These beings will now take a direct role in the affairs of Man, and, indeed, it seems that such is needed in our critical age.

The Lama and I (and that was about twenty years ago) often discussed the need of the Star People, as you call them, to come together again, to realize their affinity to each other.

Being a Star Person should never be a claim. Rather, it should be a reality from the depths of one's being—a knowing that another one is a brother or a sister in a special sense.

The link can only be ascertained within oneself. Therein there can be no lies or suppositions. One cannot fake on the inner plane a quality which one does not possess.

Therefore, the Star People on Earth have a problem which will eventually be solved through a feeling of unity with each other. Their recognition of each other will be from within.

The following is what Francie has received on love, Star Unions, and Soul Mates:

There will be many gatherings together of people during the Eighties and Nineties, and a great division will be noted. Star People will unite with one another, and Earthlings will join likewise in number. However, a truth-teaching must be realized. It must be known that when two or more people gather together, a life force comes into being, a part of God exists between them.

When two or more people come together for any *one* purpose, a life force is created. The life they bring into existence becomes separate unto itself, be it a marriage, family, company, city, state, or nation. This entity has a birthdate that is subject to astrological systems.

Each member of those who have "come together" must give to and take from the created entity in equal measure to maintain the entity's balance, existence, and health. If the members of the unit do not give and take in equal portions, a gradual depletion exists that will cause starvation, illness, and, ultimately, death of the entity.

This law remains true regardless of the nature of the entity created by the "coming together." This death may be called by many names according to the created entity—divorce, separation, bankruptcy, revolution, economic collapse, or national destruction.

The teaching may be easier to understand on a personal level, such as a man and a woman who enter into a relationship and create a "family" entity. If any members of that unit do not give and take in equal measure, then other family members must give twice as much to keep the entity alive. If the sacrificing members of the family tire and cease to give more than their share, starvation of the entity begins. If the lax members do not once again give in equal measure, the family entity will ultimately die.

Correspondingly, if the balance is maintained, then the life force grows stronger and the family is blessed by God, the ultimate life force.

The teaching applies equally on massive scale. Think of all that a nation has to give to its people: vast natural resources, metals, fuels, crops, etc. If a small minority take from these resources and hoard for personal gain, an imbalance will occur. And if through lying, illegal tax shelters, or hidden profits, they fail to return to the nation that which they have taken, the "national entity" will become weaker and weaker, until starvation occurs. If others are not overtaxed to compensate for the difference made by the profiteers, the weakened, depleted nation will eventually die.

"Throughout all of history one can see the handiwork of the Star People," Francie remarked. "They have utilized the creative arts and the sciences so they might better affect the lives of the masses. Through plays, books, poems, paintings, sculpture—and now, motion pictures and television—as well as particular architectural designs, they have affected the mass mind and caused it to recognize the possibilities of realities beyond the physical one. Creative energy, utilized in a positive manner, acknowledges its contact with the Source and seeks primarily to raise the consciousness of all humankind.

"The Starsower's plan, to aid humankind and to glorify the Source, is coming to the apex, to the peak of its mission. Throughout history, the Star People have given unselfishly of themselves for the cause of elevating their common species.

"In the past, the Star People have nearly always acted singly or in very small groups. Today, they are uniting in numbers that will be able to affect an even greater change in the awareness of all humankind. The Star People are very much aware that Earth, being physical, is intermeshed in the frequency of cause and effect, and because of this, it is about to undergo a great, transitional shaking, which will involve and evolve the entire planet."

The Star People are being more fully activated now, so that those who wish to survive the coming cataclysms and woeful devastations will be led to safe places. Here, they will heed even those admonitions from their guide which prescribe what to eat and what to drink.

The time is nearly upon Earth when great tribulations will be felt on every level.

Those who are aware, those who are in contact with their Higher Selves, will "feel" those areas on Earth which possess the greatest amounts of negativity.

Those who have received attunement will sense the most dangerous areas, and they will accomplish migrations which will lead to their survival.

Those who have learned to heed their multidimensional guides will begin to gather together for safety's sake, and they will be directed to certain places of peace and comfort.

The Star People know that they are here to aid all those who wish to evolutionize themselves on an accelerated frequency rate. They are manifesting in order to help all those who wish to survive, who desire to become Star People, and inherit the beautiful New Age that will soon come into physical being.

"We are living in a time when those who are alike must join together so that we may survive in greater numbers," Francie has said.

"Like is attracting like. No longer will the Star People be magnetically drawn to troubled areas or to troubled people in order to affect a change. The Star People are now reflecting their Higher Selves, their Souls.

"Each person is but a fragment of his or her Soul," she continued. "On its own, this physical fragment is incapable of true, unconditional love. It is submerged in ego and lacks the higher vibrations of awareness. It is insensitive to the needs of others. It must learn ways to reflect its Higher Self, its Soul.

"In the present conditions which exist, very few physical fragments reflect their Soul, but for those who do, it is the ideal state of being; and it is usually the result of a great deal of effort having been expended by the fragment in attaining the higher vibrations of love, wisdom, and knowledge."

Love is not just a relationship to a particular individual or to any living thing, Francie has been told. Love is the highest vibration which exists on Earth. If we do not feel universal love for all of life, then we may be attached to another for a variety of reasons. To feel love for even one person fully, one must possess universal love for all.

Love is the power of life, the highest frequency available to humankind. Love governs all that is and flows through the many dimensions with their myriad lifeforms. Love, truly, is God.

If you *truly* feel love for one person, you have love for all; you love the entire world, all of life. If you cannot feel such love for all living things, then you are merely attached to another lifeform for reasons of inadequacy or fear.

"Our Higher Self continuously attempts to reflect through us, so that there can be more learning gained through experience on Earth," Francie said. "On the physical plane, reflecting one's Soul can have its drawbacks, for it is extremely difficult to find like-minded fragments. Those who do reflect their Higher Selves become appalled at the anger, hatred, disrespect, and ugly behavior of the fragments who live without awareness of their Soul. Therefore, those who reflect Soul often become lonely, bewildered, and unable to share the true depth of their loving ways and their beautiful thoughts. They feel unfulfilled, and they find no relationship that is total."

Erotic love is the expression that most easily confuses, Francie has been shown. It is deceptive love. Erotic love is experienced when one individual meets another, when two strangers come together and a "spark" is ignited. Erotic love is often generated when opposites attract.

Erotic love is not a lasting expression of love. It exists only as long as the fire which has been created by the spark survives. Once intimacy has been exhausted, the passion of fiery love becomes extinguished.

The results of such unions are painful for both individuals involved. Being opposites in goals and in interests causes one or the other to become subjugated to the will of the other. Or if both personalities are strong, the fruit of a union founded on erotic love can be the abuse of one of the parties, to the detriment of the children, as well as the weaker partner.

Once the attraction of the polarities of opposites disappears, the flame of erotic love usually dies. With physical passion spent, there remain no more barriers to conquer, no further territories to explore. Those who have exhausted erotic love in such a relationship are then compelled to move on to new "opposites," with whom they can enjoy the fleeting rewards of an erotic union.

A true and a lasting love is possible between two people who truly communicate with each other. It is the type of love that grows. It can fully exist between two individuals who reflect their Higher Selves, their Soul.

"It was no happenstance that Brad and I joined together," Francie once told a couple who were interviewing her for a magazine feature article. "With my contact with Kihief, my receiving of insights and guidance, what greater, more positive relationship could there be than with one who, since earliest childhood, has felt a commitment to reach the multitudes through books. Brad has wished, in his own way, to wipe out the plagues of ignorance and the lack of awareness which threaten forever to enslave humankind.

"Brad and I were drawn together to fulfill our purpose in being. We are alike in our beliefs, our goals, our sense of mission, and our dedication to raising the consciousness of all humankind. We try always to practice reflecting our Soul."

The difference between the two types of love that result in either erotic unions or star unions, is depicted in a poem Francie channelled:

LOVE'S DIFFERENCE

When 'tis not love, but merely passion,
It gnaws with hunger deep within
And feeds upon the nearest flesh
And leaves one empty once again.

For want of comfort stirred the longing.
And fears in life did spur it all,
The seeking of a true love feeling,
And no one answering to the call.

But when 'tis love a glow does grow,
That emanates from heart and soul,
And fills one's limbs in expanding fashion,
Far surpassing normal passion,
And reaches forth as an endless river
'Til there's no line 'tween receiver and giver,
Scattering itself cross all life's scenes,
Fulfilling lovers' hopes and dreams.

"Since the Soul vibrates in a realm far superior to our own and since it has learned from its many expressions of living, it is more capable of knowing and of expressing the higher, unconditional love vibration", Francie said. True love never stagnates in an atmosphere where two or more people are becoming more aware and expanding in consciousness. Love that reflects Soul permits two individuals to work together toward a common goal, to blend to aid all of life, to merge for the purpose of one day uniting with the Source.

"Those who permit their Higher Selves to reflect through them have evolutionized beyond that of the normal expectancy rate of awareness. They have a wider perspective. They possess a part of themselves in the spiritual realm of the stars, and yet they remain aware of the lessons and the growth experiences available on Earth. They have become Star People.

"Anyone who wishes to do so may become a Star

Person. There are no exclusive qualifications which would seek to limit a person because of ethnic group, race, nationality, educational background, or religious preference. All that is required of an individual is a sincere desire to grow in awareness and to reach a Greater Reality.

"Those who sincerely seek to express their Higher Selves will begin to gather in spiritual communities where like will attract like, where they can live together in peace and harmony, where they can pursue common interests and grow in unity. These communities will be self-contained and self-sustaining."

Francie has foreseen the majority of such spiritual villages as being located beneath the surface of Earth.

"Natural and man-made underground caverns will be used for large-scale New Age communities," she has said. "These solarized 'Terra Towns' will feature low-cost, low-energy temperature control; unpolluted, filtered, oxygen-laden air; nearly total resistance to all weather factors; long-lasting protection against radioactive fallout; and all built-in appliances and furnishings. And, of course, the people will have used their intuitive abilities to build these communities away from the danger areas of the approaching cataclysms.

"These totally self-sustaining communities will have shopping malls, well-lighted walks and streets, battery-operated carts for mobility, parks and playgrounds, spas with ultraviolet 'tanning' centers, hospitals, police departments, and city-wide garbage converters which will produce energy from the community's waste.

"Few people will need to surface, with the exception of those who choose to work 'topside.' For many inhabitants, vacations will involve visiting Earth's surface.

"These will be the communities sought after and shared by the Star People, the survivors and inheritors of the New Age. These will be the villages inhabited by those who reflect their Soul.

"The evolved, Soul-reflecting fragments will join one another in physical relationships, and the joy that will come from such Soul Unions will be without boundaries. Male and female counterparts will truly share and expand in all their thoughts, words, actions, deeds, and goals. They will understand the full meaning of the blessing, 'And they shall become as one flesh.' They will be the true Soul Mates.

"As these Star Unions become whole and experience the heights of true ecstasy, they will go forth to accomplish many things that will benefit all humankind. They will strive ceaselessly to raise the consciousness and the awareness of all men and women on this planet. They will be tireless in their efforts to insure humankind's continued existence and to assure the progression of the entire species toward a rebirth in the stars and a return to the Source of All That Is."

Index